D. H. LAWRENCE

Selected Poems

EDITED, WITH AN INTRODUCTION

BY KEITH SAGAR

PENGUIN BOOKS

B
1

Penguin Books Ltd, Harmondsworth, Middlesex, England
Penguin Books, 625 Madison Avenue, New York, New York 10022, U.S.A.
Penguin Books Australia Ltd, Ringwood, Victoria, Australia
Penguin Books Canada Ltd, 2801 John Street, Markham, Ontario, Canada L3R 1B4
Penguin Books (N.Z.) Ltd, 182–190 Wairau Road, Auckland 10, New Zealand

—

This selection first published in Penguin Books 1972
Reprinted 1973
Reprinted with minor revisions 1975
Reprinted 1976, 1977, 1978, 1979

—

Copyright © the Estate of D. H. Lawrence, 1972
Introduction © Keith Sagar, 1972
All rights reserved

—

Made and printed in Great Britain by
Hazell Watson & Viney Ltd,
Aylesbury, Bucks
Set in Monotype Garamond

CONTENTS

Nettles and *More Pansies* 1929

Last Poems 1929

9

INTRODUCTION

The very scope of Lawrence's achievement in so many other forms – fiction, travel-writing, essays, criticism, letters, and plays – has told against his standing as a poet. We have come to think of his poetry as something of a by-product of, or relaxation from, other more strenuous and important work. Though it certainly came more easily than his fiction, I am sure that, except perhaps in *Pansies*, Lawrence did not think of his poetry in this way. At the outset of his career he devoted much time and care to his poems and cherished them when written. And at three subsequent periods of his life his poetry became the primary channel of his experience and creative energy: the first year of his relationship with Frieda (*Look! We Have Come Through!*), the two years in Sicily (*Birds, Beasts and Flowers*), and the last year of his life (*More Pansies* and *Last Poems*).

Lawrence wrote nearly 1,000 poems, and we must concede that an unusually high proportion are unsuccessful. He needs to be read in selection. Reviewing Lawrence's *Complete Poems*, D. J. Enright wrote:

It must be granted that this *Complete Poems* – however grateful many of us will be to have it – makes for oppressive, confusing and blunted reading. There is still room for a critical selection; none of those I have seen conveys a true sense of the fantastic variety and scope of Lawrence's verse.

I have tried to fill this gap. Moreover, I have tried to bring together in one volume all Lawrence's really successful, achieved poems – the poems on which his claim to the status of a major poet must rest.

I believe that on the strength of these 150 poems we can support the claim that Lawrence is a great poet in every sense, including the technical. The technique for making something out of nothing he had not, nor the technique of highly finished formal craftsmanship. Such technique might have improved some of his early poems. It might equally have prevented him going on to write the great poems, where the form is the perfect incarnation of the content, the perfect vehicle for the liveliness of thought and feeling, the freshness and depth of perception, the wit and wisdom he has to offer.

Many of the early poems printed here are in versions different from those with which the reader may be familiar. Lawrence extensively revised, and in some cases rewrote, these poems when preparing his *Collected Poems* in 1928. In his introductory note to that edition Lawrence says that he has tried to establish a chronological order,

because many of the poems are so personal that, in their fragmentary fashion, they make up a biography of an emotional and inner life.

Yet he goes on to say that some are

a good deal rewritten. They were struggling to say something which it takes a man twenty years to be able to say ... A young man is afraid of his demon and puts his hand over the demon's mouth sometimes and speaks for him. And the things the young man says are very rarely poetry. So I have tried to let the demon say his say, and to remove the passages where the young man intruded.

The result, even when the poems are improved, which is not always, is a kind of ventriloquism, with the voice of the mature Lawrence speaking, sometimes grotesquely, through the mouth of the dumb young man. How ridiculous, for example, to suppose that the young man of twenty-two, out of his actual virginity, could have written the version of *Virgin Youth* which appears in the *Collected Poems*. It is a poem by the author of *Lady Chatterley's Lover*. It seems to me much more important that we should have what the young man actually wrote at twenty-two than what Lawrence at forty-two (a much better poet, but a different man with a different demon) thought he should have written. I have therefore taken the texts from *Love Poems*, *Amores*, *New Poems* and *Bay* where they first appeared in book form.

The earliest poems date from the period 1906–8 when Lawrence was a student at Nottingham University College. The girl who figures in many of them is his first sweetheart, Jessie Chambers, the Miriam of *Sons and Lovers*. The rest of the early poems were written between 1908 and 1911, when Lawrence was teaching in Croydon. The best of them are distinguished by what Alfred Alvarez has called Lawrence's 'emotional realism'. Candour, truth and power of feeling often burst through the conventional frame in startling imagery: the voices of the parents in his childhood remembered as slender and thick lashes competing with the terrible whips of the ash-tree outside, shrieking in a storm at night; cherries hanging round the ears of a girl seen as blood-drops, thus linking her offer of love with the dead birds under the cherry tree; sex and violence again linked by potent imagery in *Renascence*, *Snap-Dragon* and *Cruelty and Love*; striking images of light and dark, colour and movement; images which presage the mature Lawrence – rainbows, dolphins, the long sea journey through 'the grandeur of night' to the amazing newness of dawn, resurrection, and the return to Paradise.

In 1913 Lawrence wrote to Edward Marsh:

I have always tried to get an emotion out in its own course, without altering it. It needs the finest instinct imaginable, much finer than the skill of the craftsmen . . . I don't write for your ear . . . I can't tell you what *pattern* I see in any poetry, save one complete thing.

But Lawrence's instinct, at this stage of his career, worked fitfully, and there was little craftsmanship to fall back on. He had no ear for formal rhythm or rhyme, and when he attempted them was usually inept.

Occasionally, in these early poems, the rhythm briefly frees itself and springs to life:

Rabbits, handfuls of brown earth, lie
Low-rounded on the mournful grass they have bitten down to the
    quick.
Are they asleep? – Are they alive? – Now see, when I
Move my arms the hill bursts and heaves under their spurting kick.

Sometimes he achieves the moving colloquial directness and simplicity of Brecht:

But when I meet the weary eyes
The reddened, aching eyes of the bar-man with thin arms,
I am glad to go back where I came from.

Particularly impressive are the four dialect poems, on the strength of which Pound proposed Lawrence for the Polignac Prize. Here Lawrence is able to forget Swinburne, Meredith and the Pre-Raphaelites and take his rhythms from the local speech he knew so well.

Lawrence never shied from sentiment for fear of sentimentality. He had the courage of his emotions, whether grief for the dead mother, sexual frustration, nostalgia for childhood, or delight in the baby which ran across the lawn to him. He expressed them all with rare delicacy. But they were the emotions of a man who had not found himself and who was at odds with his life.

Lawrence came to maturity as a poet at the same time that he came to maturity as a man and a novelist, at the time of his marriage. It is as though the new life which he launched with Frieda in 1912 and his departure from England freed him from the pressures which had retarded his development and the conventions which had crippled so much of his verse. *Look! We Have Come Through!* is a record of his early years with Frieda, up to the war. It is also an epithalamium, a celebration of love and marriage, not omitting the conflict and occasional misery. Marriage, Lawrence claimed, 'sort of keeps me in direct communication with the unknown, in which otherwise I am a bit lost'. His vision becomes increasingly sacramental. He does not distinguish between the creativeness which brings him and Frieda through to 'some condition of blessedness', and the creativeness which issues in poetry; neither is an achievement of the deliberate self, both are products of the wind that blows through him to which he must open and attune himself:

> Oh, for the wonder that bubbles into my soul
> I would be a good fountain, a good well-head,
> Would blur no whisper, spoil no expression.

The success of his marriage is achieved by breaking through old dead ideas and life-modes. In his art, too, he seeks to break down all the 'artificial conduits and canals through which we do so love to force our utterance', to allow the spontaneous, uniquely appropriate form to emerge. This technique produces, when successful (as it is increasingly to be), 'the perfect utterance of a concentrated spontaneous soul'. It is a far deeper and more demanding discipline than the discipline of the craftsman. Lawrence has no use for the word 'aesthetic'. The discipline is spiritual and emotional as well as linguistic. The poems are a by-product of 'that piece of supreme art, a man's life'. Some of the poems in *Look!* are personal in the restricting sense. But it is only through the wholeness and depth of personal experience that Lawrence is to create the impersonally authentic forms and universal meanings of *Birds, Beasts and Flowers*.

The horrors of the war, the moral debacle at home, the suppression of his splendid novel, *The Rainbow*, persecution, ill-health and poverty, all combined to destroy in Lawrence, during the war, his faith in humanity and a human future. He turned, to retain his sanity and faith in life, to the non-human world of birds, beasts and flowers.

Lawrence had an almost occult penetration into the being of other creatures. But in several of the best poems, the purpose is to reveal the sheer unknowable otherness of the non-human life and its strange gods. He goes to the very pale of his being, of human consciousness, and looks outward. Creatures, 'little living myths', bring him messages not only from out of the surrounding darkness, but also from the unknown depths of his own being:

In the very darkest continent of the body there is God. And from Him issue the first dark rays of our feeling, wordless, and utterly previous to words: the innermost rays, the first messengers, the primeval, honourable beasts of our being, whose voice echoes wordless and forever wordless down the darkest avenues of the soul, but full of potent speech. Our own inner meaning.

Lawrence is here making his own raid on the inarticulate. And the messengers he comes nearest to understanding are the snake and the tortoise. *Tortoises* is one long poem in six sections, a metaphysical poem about the tragedy of man's sexuality, with all the suffering, dependence, exposure that implies, and yet, ultimately, the joy, for it is a means, like death, to marriage with the universe.

There is no longer, in *Birds, Beasts and Flowers*, any sign of formal difficulty. Lawrence's demon, his daring visionary insight, speaks out clear and bold (though somewhat stridently in the less successful poems). Ostensibly about creatures, these poems explore a vast range of experience. They are dramatic confrontations between the human and non-human and potent evocations of the spirit of place. They are brimming with vitality and awareness, humour and wisdom.

Lawrence called his next volume *Pansies* because the poems are little thoughts like Pascal's *Pensées*, and because he wanted them to be thought of as unpretentious flowers blooming briefly, rather jauntily, not as monuments for posterity. He called them 'rag poems'. In the best of them we hear what Richard Hoggart has called 'the voice of a down-to-earth, tight, bright, witty Midlander ... slangy, quick, flat and direct, lively, laconic, sceptical, non-conforming, nicely bloody-minded'. The less successful are merely 'sketches for poems', or, like the pieces of soft fruit Ibsen gave his pet scorpion, something into which Lawrence could discharge his accumulated venom.

In *More Pansies* and *Last Poems* Lawrence's thoughts become poems much more consistently than in *Pansies*. Thought is 'a man in his wholeness wholly attending' and here the poet strives to make 'a new act of attention' and then give 'direct utterance from the instant, whole man' in language that will make us prick our innermost ear. His primary theme is life's tremendous characterization and man's capacity for wonder. Now, on the brink of death, he gives us the naïve opening of a soul to life. Despite his awareness of the desperate ills of our civilization and of his own impending death, he is no longer, as he often was in *Pansies*, flippant or exasperated or spiteful. His new-found insouciance brings assurance, playfulness, and a new joy in life, in 'the magnificent here and now of life in the flesh'. It is a kind of resurrection as the dying tree puts out new strange blossoms.

The clarity and splendour of these poems testifies to the depth of vision they spring from – what Coleridge meant when he spoke of Wordsworth's 'sentiments':

No frequency of perusal can deprive them of their freshness. For though they are brought into the full daylight of every reader's comprehension; yet are they drawn up from depths which few in any age are privileged to visit, into which few in any age have courage to descend.

This courage manifests itself supremely in *Bavarian Gentians* and the other poems about death. They are poignant, but never waver in their faith that death is only a part of life, the longest journey, perhaps the greatest adventure.

Early Poems

DISCORD IN CHILDHOOD

OUTSIDE the house an ash-tree hung its terrible whips,
And at night when the wind arose, the lash of the tree
Shrieked and slashed the wind, as a ship's
Weird rigging in a storm shrieks hideously.

Within the house two voices arose in anger, a slender lash
Whistling delirious rage, and the dreadful sound
Of a thick lash booming and bruising, until it drowned
The other voice in a silence of blood, 'neath the noise of
 the ash.

PIANO

SOFTLY, in the dusk, a woman is singing to me;
Taking me back down the vista of years, till I see
A child sitting under the piano, in the boom of the tingling
 strings
And pressing the small, poised feet of a mother who smiles
 as she sings.

In spite of myself, the insidious mastery of song
Betrays me back, till the heart of me weeps to belong
To the old Sunday evenings at home, with winter outside
And hymns in the cosy parlour, the tinkling piano our
 guide.

So now it is vain for the singer to burst into clamour
With the great black piano appassionato. The glamour
Of childish days is upon me, my manhood is cast
Down in the flood of remembrance, I weep like a child for
 the past.

THE WILD COMMON

THE quick sparks on the gorse bushes are leaping,
Little jets of sunlight-texture imitating flame;
Above them, exultant, the peewits are sweeping:
They are lords of the desolate wastes of sadness their
    screamings proclaim.

Rabbits, handfuls of brown earth, lie
Low-rounded on the mournful grass they have bitten down
    to the quick.
Are they asleep? – Are they alive? – Now see, when I
Move my arms the hill bursts and heaves under their
    spurting kick.

The common flaunts bravely; but below, from the rushes
Crowds of glittering king-cups surge to challenge the
    blossoming bushes;
There the lazy streamlet pushes
Its curious course mildly; here it wakes again, leaps, laughs,
    and gushes

Into a deep pond, an old sheep-dip,
Dark, overgrown with willows, cool, with the brook
    ebbing through so slow;
Naked on the steep, soft lip
Of the bank I stand watching my own white shadow
    quivering to and fro.

What if the gorse flowers shrivelled and kissing were lost?
Without the pulsing waters, where were the marigolds and
    the songs of the brook?
If my veins and my breasts with love embossed
Withered, my insolent soul would be gone like flowers that
    the hot wind took.

So my soul like a passionate woman turns,
Filled with remorseful terror to the man she scorned,
    and her love
For myself in my own eyes' laughter burns,
Runs ecstatic over the pliant folds rippling down to my
    belly from the breast-lights above.

Over my sunlit skin the warm, clinging air,
Rich with the songs of seven larks singing at once,
    goes kissing me glad.
And the soul of the wind and my blood compare
Their wandering happiness, and the wind, wasted in liberty,
    drifts on and is sad.

Oh but the water loves me and folds me,
Plays with me, sways me, lifts me and sinks me as though
    it were living blood,
Blood of a heaving woman who holds me,
Owning my supple body a rare glad thing, supremely good.

CHERRY ROBBERS

UNDER the long, dark boughs, like jewels red
    In the hair of an Eastern girl
Shine strings of crimson cherries, as if had bled
    Blood-drops beneath each curl.

Under the glistening cherries, with folded wings
    Three dead birds lie:
Pale-breasted throstles and a blackbird, robberlings
    Stained with red dye.

Under the haystack a girl stands laughing at me,
    With cherries hung round her ears –
Offering me her scarlet fruit: I will see
    If she has any tears.

WE have bit no forbidden apple,
    Eve and I,
Yet the splashes of day and night
Falling round us no longer dapple
The same Eden with purple and white.

This is our own still valley
    Our Eden, our home,
But day shows it vivid with feeling
And the pallor of night does not tally
With dark sleep that once covered its ceiling.

My little red heifer, to-night I looked in her eyes,
    – She will calve to-morrow:

Last night when I went with the lantern, the sow was
    grabbing her litter
With red, snarling jaws: and I heard the cries
Of the new-born, and after that, the old owl, then the bats
    that flitter.

And I woke to the sound of the wood-pigeons, and lay and
    listened,
    Till I could borrow
A few quick beats of a wood-pigeon's heart, and when I
    did rise
The morning sun on the shaken iris glistened,
And I saw that home, this valley, was wider than Paradise.

I learned it all from my Eve
    This warm, dumb wisdom.
She's a finer instructress than years;
She has taught my heart-strings to weave
Through the web of all laughter and tears.

And now I see the valley
    Fleshed all like me
With feelings that change and quiver:
And all things seem to tally
    With something in me,
Something of which she's the giver.

SNAP-DRAGON

She bade me follow to her garden, where
The mellow sunlight stood as in a cup
Between the old grey walls; I did not dare
To raise my face, I did not dare look up,
Lest her bright eyes like sparrows should fly in
My windows of discovery, and shrill 'Sin.'

So with a downcast mien and laughing voice
I followed, followed the swing of her white dress
That rocked in a lilt along: I watched the poise
Of her feet as they flew for a space, then paused to press
The grass deep down with the royal burden of her:
And gladly I'd offered my breast to the tread of her.

'I like to see,' she said, and she crouched her down,
She sunk into my sight like a settling bird;
And her bosom couched in the confines of her gown
Like heavy birds at rest there, softly stirred
By her measured breaths: 'I like to see,' said she,
'The snap-dragon put out his tongue at me.'

She laughed, she reached her hand out to the flower,
Closing its crimson throat. My own throat in her power
Strangled, my heart swelled up so full
As if it would burst its wine-skin in my throat,
Choke me in my own crimson. I watched her pull
The gorge of the gaping flower, till the blood did float

Over my eyes, and I was blind –
Her large brown hand stretched over
The windows of my mind;
And there in the dark I did discover
Things I was out to find:
My Grail, a brown bowl twined
With swollen veins that met in the wrist,
Under whose brown the amethyst
I longed to taste. I longed to turn
My heart's red measure in her cup,
I longed to feel my hot blood burn
With the amethyst in her cup.

Then suddenly she looked up,
And I was blind in a tawny-gold day,
Till she took her eyes away.

So she came down from above
And emptied my heart of love.
So I held my heart aloft
To the cuckoo that hung like a dove,
And she settled soft.

It seemed that I and the morning world
Were pressed cup-shape to take this reiver
Bird who was weary to have furled
Her wings in us,
As we were weary to receive her.

> *This bird, this rich,*
> *Sumptuous central grain,*
> *This mutable witch,*
> *This one refrain,*
> *This laugh in the fight,*
> *This clot of night,*
> *This field of delight.*

She spoke, and I closed my eyes
To shut hallucinations out.
I echoed with surprise
Hearing my mere lips shout
The answer they did devise.

Again I saw a brown bird hover
Over the flowers at my feet;
I felt a brown bird hover
Over my heart, and sweet
Its shadow lay on my heart.
I thought I saw on the clover
A brown bee pulling apart
The closed flesh of the clover
And burrowing in its heart.

She moved her hand, and again
I felt the brown bird cover
My heart; and then
The bird came down on my heart,
As on a nest the rover
Cuckoo comes, and shoves over
The brim each careful part
Of love, takes possession, and settles her down,
With her wings and her feathers to drown
The nest in a heat of love.

She turned her flushed face to me for the glint
Of a moment. 'See,' she laughed, 'if you also
Can make them yawn.' I put my hand to the dint
In the flower's throat, and the flower gaped wide with woe.
She watched, she went of a sudden intensely still,
She watched my hand, to see what it would fulfil.

I pressed the wretched, throttled flower between
My fingers, till its head lay back, its fangs
Poised at her. Like a weapon my hand was white and keen,

And I held the choked flower-serpent in its pangs
Of mordant anguish, till she ceased to laugh,
Until her pride's flag, smitten, cleaved down to the staff.

She hid her face, she murmured between her lips
The low word 'Don't.' I let the flower fall,
But held my hand afloat towards the slips
Of blossom she fingered, and my fingers all
Put forth to her: she did not move, nor I,
For my hand like a snake watched hers, that could not fly.

Then I laughed in the dark of my heart, I did exult
Like a sudden chuckling of music. I bade her eyes
Meet mine, I opened her helpless eyes to consult
Their fear, their shame, their joy that underlies
Defeat in such a battle. In the dark of her eyes
My heart was fierce to make her laughter rise.

Till her dark deeps shook with convulsive thrills, and the
    dark
Of her spirit wavered like water thrilled with light;
And my heart leaped up in longing to plunge its stark
Fervour within the pool of her twilight,
Within her spacious soul, to find delight.

And I do not care, though the large hands of revenge
Shall get my throat at last, shall get it soon,
If the joy that they are lifted to avenge
Have risen red on my night as a harvest moon,
Which even death can only put out for me;
And death, I know, is better than not-to-be.

CRUELTY AND LOVE

WHAT large, dark hands are those at the window
Lifted, grasping the golden light
Which weaves its way through the creeper leaves
        To my heart's delight?

28

Ah, only the leaves! But in the west,
In the west I see a redness come
Over the evening's burning breast –
      – 'Tis the wound of love goes home!

  The woodbine creeps abroad
  Calling low to her lover:
    The sun-lit flirt who all the day
    Has poised above her lips in play
    And stolen kisses, shallow and gay
    Of pollen, now has gone away
    – She woos the moth with her sweet, low word,
  And when above her his broad wings hover
  Then her bright breast she will uncover
  And yield her honey-drop to her lover.

Into the yellow, evening glow
Saunters a man from the farm below,
Leans, and looks in at the low-built shed
Where hangs the swallow's marriage bed.
    The bird lies warm against the wall.
    She glances quick her startled eyes
    Towards him, then she turns away
    Her small head, making warm display
    Of red upon the throat. His terrors sway
  Her out of the nest's warm, busy ball,
  Whose plaintive cry is heard as she flies
  In one blue stoop from out the sties
  Into the evening's empty hall.

Oh, water-hen, beside the rushes
Hide your quaint, unfading blushes,
Still your quick tail, and lie as dead,
Till the distance folds over his ominous tread.

The rabbit presses back her ears,
Turns back her liquid, anguished eyes

29

And crouches low: then with wild spring
Spurts from the terror of *his* oncoming
To be choked back, the wire ring
Her frantic effort throttling:
    Piteous brown ball of quivering fears!

Ah soon in his large, hard hands she dies,
And swings all loose to the swing of his walk.
Yet calm and kindly are his eyes
And ready to open in brown surprise
Should I not answer to his talk
Or should he my tears surmise.

I hear his hand on the latch, and rise from my chair
Watching the door open: he flashes bare
His strong teeth in a smile, and flashes his eyes
In a smile like triumph upon me; then careless-wise
He flings the rabbit soft on the table board
And comes towards me: ah, the uplifted sword
Of his hand against my bosom, and oh, the broad
Blade of his hand that raises my face to applaud
His coming: he raises up my face to him
And caresses my mouth with his fingers, which still smell
    grim
Of the rabbit's fur! God, I am caught in a snare!
I know not what fine wire is round my throat,
I only know I let him finger there
My pulse of life, letting him nose like a stoat
Who sniffs with joy before he drinks the blood:
And down his mouth comes to my mouth, and down
His dark bright eyes descend like a fiery hood
Upon my mind: his mouth meets mine, and a flood
Of sweet fire sweeps across me, so I drown
Within him, die, and find death good.

GIPSY

I, THE man with the red scarf,
    Will give thee what I have, this last week's earnings.
Take them, and buy thee a silver ring
    And wed me, to ease my yearnings.

For the rest, when thou art wedded
    I'll wet my brow for thee
With sweat, I'll enter a house for thy sake,
    Thou shalt shut doors on me.

A COLLIER'S WIFE

SOMEBODY'S knocking at the door
    Mother, come down and see.
– I's think it's nobbut a beggar,
    Say, I'm busy.

It's not a beggar, mother, – hark
    How hard he knocks . . .
– Eh, tha'rt a mard-'arsed kid,
    'E'll gi'e thee socks!

Shout an' ax what 'e wants,
    I canna come down.
– 'E says 'Is it Arthur Holliday's?'
    Say 'Yes,' tha clown.

'E says, 'Tell your mother as 'er mester's
    Got hurt i' th' pit.'
What – oh my sirs, 'e never says that,
    That's niver it.

Come out o' the way an' let me see,
    Eh, there's no peace!
An' stop thy scraightin', childt,
    Do shut thy face.

'Your mester's 'ad an accident,
    An' they're ta'ein 'im i' th' ambulance
To Nottingham,' – Eh dear o' me
    If 'e's not a man for mischance!

Wheers he hurt this time, lad?
    – I dunna know,
They on'y towd me it wor bad –
    It would be so!

Eh, what a man! – an' that cobbly road,
    They'll jolt him a'most to death,
I'm sure he's in for some trouble
    Nigh every time he takes breath.

Out o' my way, childt – dear o' me, wheer
    Have I put his clean stockings and shirt;
Goodness knows if they'll be able
    To take off his pit dirt.

An' what a moan he'll make – there niver
    Was such a man for a fuss
If anything ailed him – at any rate
    I shan't have him to nuss.

I do hope it's not very bad!
    Eh, what a shame it seems
As some should ha'e hardly a smite o' trouble
    An' others has reams.

It's a shame as 'e should be knocked about
    Like this, I'm sure it is!
He's had twenty accidents, if he's had one;
    Owt bad, an' it's his.

There's one thing, we'll have peace for a bit,
    Thank Heaven for a peaceful house;
An' there's compensation, sin' it's accident,
    An' club money – I nedn't grouse.

An' a fork an' a spoon he'll want, an' what else;
    I s'll never catch that train –
What a traipse it is if a man gets hurt –
    I s'd think he'll get right again.

VIOLETS

SISTER, tha knows while we was on the planks
    Aside o' th' grave, while th' coffin wor lyin' yet
On th' yaller clay, an' th' white flowers top of it
    Tryin' to keep off 'n him a bit o' th' wet,

An' parson makin' haste, an' a' the black
    Huddlin' close together a cause o' th' rain,
Did t' 'appen ter notice a bit of a lass away back
    By a head-stun, sobbin' an' sobbin' again?

    – How should I be looking' round
        An' me standin' on the plank
    Beside the open ground,
        Where our Ted 'ud soon be sank?

    Yi, an' 'im that young,
        Snapped sudden out of all
    His wickedness, among
        Pals worse n'r ony name as you could call.

Let be that; there's some o' th' bad as we
    Like better nor all your good, an' 'e was one.
– An' cos I liked him best, yi, bett'r nor thee,
    I canna bide to think where he is gone.

Ah know tha liked 'im bett'r nor me. But let
    Me tell thee about this lass. When you had gone
Ah stopped behind on t' pad i' th' drippin wet
    An' watched what 'er 'ad on.

33

Tha should ha' seed 'er slive up when we'd gone,
  Tha should ha' seed her kneel an' look in
At th' sloppy wet grave – an' 'er little neck shone
  That white, an' 'er shook that much, I'd like to begin

Scraightin' mysen as well. 'Er undid 'er black
  Jacket at th' bosom, an' took from out of it
Over a double 'andful of violets, all in a pack
  Ravelled blue and white – warm, for a bit

O' th' smell come waftin' to me. 'Er put 'er face
  Right intil 'em and scraighted out again,
Then after a bit 'er dropped 'em down that place,
  An' I come away, because o' the teemin' rain.

DREAMS OLD AND NASCENT

Old

I HAVE opened the window to warm my hands on the sill
Where the sunlight soaks in the stone: the afternoon
Is full of dreams, my love, the boys are all still
In a wistful dream of Lorna Doone.

The clink of the shunting engines is sharp and fine,
Like savage music striking far off, and there
On the great, uplifted blue palace, lights stir and shine
Where the glass is domed in the blue, soft air.

There lies the world, my darling, full of wonder and
    wistfulness and strange
Recognitions and greetings of half-acquaint things, as I
    greet the cloud
Of blue palace aloft there, among misty indefinite dreams
    that range
At the back of my life's horizon, where the dreamings of
    past lives crowd.

Over the nearness of Norwood Hill, through the mellow
  veil
Of the afternoon glows to me the old romance of David
  and Dora,
With the old, sweet, soothing tears, and laughter that shakes
  the sail
Of the ship of the soul over seas where dreamed dreams
  lure the unoceaned explorer.

All the bygone, hushèd years
Streaming back where the mist distils
Into forgetfulness: soft-sailing waters where fears
No longer shake, where the silk sail fills
With an unfelt breeze that ebbs over the seas, where the
  storm
Of living has passed, on and on
Through the coloured iridescence that swims in the warm
Wake of the tumult now spent and gone,
Drifts my boat, wistfully lapsing after
The mists of vanishing tears and the echo of laughter.

Nascent

MY world is a painted fresco, where coloured shapes
Of old, ineffectual lives linger blurred and warm;
An endless tapestry the past has woven drapes
The halls of my life, compelling my soul to conform.

The surface of dreams is broken,
The picture of the past is shaken and scattered.
Fluent, active figures of men pass along the railway, and I
  am woken
From the dreams that the distance flattered.

Along the railway, active figures of men.
They have a secret that stirs in their limbs as they move

Out of the distance, nearer, commanding my dreamy
world.

Here in the subtle, rounded flesh
Beats the active ecstasy.
In the sudden lifting my eyes, it is clearer,
The fascination of the quick, restless Creator moving
through the mesh
Of men, vibrating in ecstasy through the rounded flesh.

Oh my boys, bending over your books,
In you is trembling and fusing
The creation of a new-patterned dream, dream of a genera-
tion:
And I watch to see the Creator, the power that patterns the
dream.

The old dreams are beautiful, beloved, soft-toned, and
sure,
But the dream-stuff is molten and moving mysteriously,
Alluring my eyes; for I, am I not also dream-stuff,
Am I not quickening, diffusing myself in the pattern, shap-
ing and shapen?

Here in my class is the answer for the great yearning:
Eyes where I can watch the swim of old dreams reflected on
the molten metal of dreams,
Watch the stir which is rhythmic and moves them all as a
heart-beat moves the blood,
Here in the swelling flesh the great activity working,
Visible there in the change of eyes and the mobile features.

Oh the great mystery and fascination of the unseen Shaper,
The power of the melting, fusing Force – heat, light, all in
one,
Everything great and mysterious in one, swelling and shap-
ing the dream in the flesh,
As it swells and shapes a bud into blossom.

Oh the terrible ecstasy of the consciousness that I am life!
Oh the miracle of the whole, the widespread, labouring
　　concentration
Swelling mankind like one bud to bring forth the fruit of a
　　dream,
Oh the terror of lifting the innermost I out of the sweep of
　　the impulse of life,
And watching the great Thing labouring through the
　　whole round flesh of the world;
And striving to catch a glimpse of the shape of the coming
　　dream,
As it quickens within the labouring, white-hot metal,
Catch the scent and the colour of the coming dream,
Then to fall back exhausted into the unconscious, molten
　　life!

AFTERNOON IN SCHOOL

The Last Lesson

WHEN will the bell ring, and end this weariness?
How long have they tugged the leash, and strained apart
My pack of unruly hounds: I cannot start
Them again on a quarry of knowledge they hate to hunt,
I can haul them and urge them no more.
No more can I endure to bear the brunt
Of the books that lie out on the desks: a full three score
Of several insults of blotted pages and scrawl
Of slovenly work that they have offered me.
I am sick, and tired more than any thrall
Upon the woodstacks working weariedly.

　　　　　　　　　　And shall I take
The last dear fuel and heap it on my soul
Till I rouse my will like a fire to consume
Their dross of indifference, and burn the scroll
Of their insults in punishment? – I will not!

I will not waste myself to embers for them,
Not all for them shall the fires of my life be hot,
For myself a heap of ashes of weariness, till sleep
Shall have raked the embers clear: I will keep
Some of my strength for myself, for if I should sell
It all for them, I should hate them –
       – I will sit and wait for the bell.

A BABY RUNNING BAREFOOT

WHEN the bare feet of the baby beat across the grass
The little white feet nod like white flowers in the wind,
They poise and run like ripples lapping across the water;
And the sight of their white play among the grass
Is like a little robin's song, winsome,
Or as two white butterflies settle in the cup of one flower
For a moment, then away with a flutter of wings.

I long for the baby to wander hither to me
Like a wind-shadow wandering over the water,
So that she can stand on my knee
With her little bare feet in my hands,
Cool like syringa buds,
Firm and silken like pink young peony flowers.

END OF ANOTHER HOME-HOLIDAY

I

WHEN shall I see the half moon sink again
Behind the black sycamore at the end of the garden?
When will the scent of the dim, white phlox
Creep up the wall to me, and in at my open window?

Why is it, the long slow stroke of the midnight bell,
    (Will it never finish the twelve?)
Falls again and again on my heart with a heavy reproach?

The moon-mist is over the village, out of the mist speaks
      the bell,
And all the little roofs of the village bow low, pitiful,
      beseeching, resigned:
    Oh, little home, what is it I have not done well?

Ah home, suddenly I love you,
As I hear the sharp clean trot of a pony down the road,
Succeeding sharp little sounds dropping into the silence,
Clear upon the long-drawn hoarseness of a train across the
      valley.

The light has gone out from under my mother's door.
        That she should love me so,
        She, so lonely, greying now,
        And I leaving her,
        Bent on my pursuits!

    Love is the great Asker,
    The sun and the rain do not ask the secret
    Of the time when the grain struggles down in the dark.
    The moon walks her lonely way without anguish,
    Because no loved one grieves over her departure.

2

Forever, ever by my shoulder pitiful Love will linger,
Crouching as little houses crouch under the mist when I
      turn.
Forever, out of the mist the church lifts up her reproachful
      finger,
Pointing my eyes in wretched defiance where love hides her
      face to mourn.

    Oh but the rain creeps down to wet the grain
        That struggles alone in the dark,
    And asking nothing, cheerfully steals back again!

The moon sets forth o' nights
To walk the lonely, dusky heights
Serenely, with steps unswerving;
Pursued by no sigh of bereavement,
No tears of love unnerving
Her constant tread:
While ever at my side,
Frail and sad, with grey bowed head,
The beggar-woman, the yearning-eyed
Inexorable love goes lagging.

The wild young heifer, glancing distraught,
With a strange new knocking of life at her side
Runs seeking a loneliness.
The little grain draws down the earth to hide.
Nay, even the slumberous egg, as it labours under the shell,
Patiently to divide, and self-divide,
Asks to be hidden, and wishes nothing to tell.

But when I draw the scanty cloak of silence over my eyes,
Piteous Love comes peering under the hood.
Touches the clasp with trembling fingers, and tries
To put her ear to the painful sob of my blood,
While her tears soak through to my breast,
Where they burn and cauterise.

3

The moon lies back and reddens.
In the valley, a corncrake calls
Monotonously,
With a piteous, unalterable plaint, that deadens
My confident activity:
With a hoarse, insistent request that falls
Unweariedly, unweariedly,
Asking something more of me,
Yet more of me!

COROT

THE trees rise tall and taller, lifted
On a subtle rush of cool grey flame
That issuing out of the dawn has sifted
  The spirit from each leaf's frame.

For the trailing, leisurely rapture of life
Drifts dimly forward, easily hidden
By bright leaves uttered aloud, and strife
  Of shapes in the grey mist chidden.

The grey, phosphorescent, pellucid advance
Of the luminous purpose of God shines out
Where the lofty trees athwart stream chance
  To shake flakes of its shadow about.

The subtle, steady rush of the whole
Grey foam-mist of advancing God,
As He silently sweeps to His somewhere, his goal,
  Is heard in the grass of the sod.

Is heard in the windless whisper of leaves
In the silent labours of men in the field,
In the downward dropping of flimsy sheaves
  Of cloud the rain skies yield.

In the tapping haste of a fallen leaf,
In the flapping of red-roof smoke, and the small
Foot-stepping tap of men beneath
  These trees so huge and tall.

For what can all sharp-rimmed substance but catch
In a backward ripple, God's purpose, reveal
For a moment His mighty direction, snatch
  A spark beneath His wheel.

Since God sweeps onward dim and vast,
Creating the channelled vein of Man
And Leaf for His passage, His shadow is cast
  On all for us to scan.

Ah listen, for Silence is not lonely:
Imitate the magnificent trees
That speak no word of their rapture, but only
  Breathe largely the luminous breeze.

AFTER THE OPERA

Down the stone stairs
Girls with their large eyes wide with tragedy
Lift looks of shocked and momentous emotions up at me.
And I smile.

Ladies
Stepping like birds with their bright and pointed feet
Peer anxiously forth, as if for a boat to carry them out of
    the wreckage,
And among the wreck of the theatre crowd
I stand and smile.

They take tragedy so becomingly.
Which pleases me.

But when I meet the weary eyes
The reddened aching eyes of the bar-man with thin arms,
I am glad to go back where I came from.

THE BRIDE

My love looks like a girl to-night,
  But she is old.
The plaits that lie along her pillow
  Are not gold,

But threaded with filigree silver,
  And uncanny cold.

She looks like a young maiden, since her brow
  Is smooth and fair,
Her cheeks are very smooth, her eyes are closed.
  She sleeps a rare
Still winsome sleep, so still, and so composed.

Nay, but she sleeps like a bride, and dreams her dreams
  Of perfect things.
She lies at last, the darling, in the shape of her dream,
  And her dead mouth sings
By its shape, like the thrushes in clear evenings.

SORROW

WHY does the thin grey strand
Floating up from the forgotten
Cigarette between my fingers,
Why does it trouble me?

Ah, you will understand;
When I carried my mother downstairs,
A few times only, at the beginning
Of her soft-foot malady,

I should find, for a reprimand
To my gaiety, a few long grey hairs
On the breast of my coat; and one by one
I watched them float up the dark chimney.

WHETHER OR NOT

I

DUNNA thee tell me its his'n, mother,
  Dunna thee, dunna thee.

– Oh ay! he'll be comin' to tell thee his-sèn
  Wench, wunna he?

Tha doesna mean to say to me, mother,
  He's gone wi that –
– My gel, owt'll do for a man i' the dark,
  Tha's got it flat.

But 'er's old, mother, 'er's twenty year
  Older nor him –
– Ay, an' yaller as a crowflower, an' yet i' the dark
  Er'd do for Tim.

Tha niver believes it, mother, does ter?
  It's somebody's lies.
– Ax him thy-sèn wench – a widder's lodger;
  It's no surprise.

2

A widow of forty-five
With a bitter, swarthy skin,
To ha' 'ticed a lad o' twenty-five
An' 'im to have been took in!

A widow of forty-five
As has sludged like a horse all her life,
Till 'er's tough as whit-leather, to slive
Atween a lad an' 'is wife!

A widow of forty-five,
A tough old otchel wi' long
Witch teeth, an' 'er black hawk-eyes as I've
Mistrusted all along!

An' me as 'as kep my-sen
Shut like a daisy bud,
Clean an' new an' nice, so's when
He wed he'd ha'e summat good!

44

An' 'im as nice an' fresh
As any man i' the force,
To ha'e gone an' given his white young flesh
To a woman that coarse!

3

You're stout to brave this snow, Miss Stainwright,
  Are you makin' Brinsley way?
— I'm off up th' line to Underwood
  Wi' a dress as is wanted to-day.

Oh are you goin' to Underwood?
  'Appen then you've 'eered?
— What's that as 'appen I've 'eered-on, Missis,
  Speak up, you nedna be feared.

Why, your young man an' Widow Naylor,
  Her as he lodges wi',
They say he's got her wi' childt; but there,
  It's nothing to do wi' me.

Though if it's true they'll turn him out
  O' th' p'lice force, without fail;
An' if it's not true, I'd back my life
  They'll listen to *her* tale.

Well, I'm believin' no tale, Missis,
  I'm seein' for my-sen;
An' when I know for sure, Missis,
  I'll talk *then*.

4

Nay robin red-breast, tha nedna
  Sit noddin' thy head at me;
My breast's as red as thine, I reckon
  Flayed red, if tha could but see.

Nay, you blessed pee-whips,
    You nedna screet at me!
I'm screetin' my-sen, but are-na goin'
    To let iv'rybody see.

Tha *art* smock-ravelled, bunny,
    Larropin' neck an' crop
I' th' snow: but I's warrant thee, bunny,
    I'm further ower th' top.

5

Now sithee theer at th' railroad crossin'
Warmin' his-sen at the stool o' fire
Under the tank as fills the ingines,
If there isn't my dearly-beloved liar!

My constable wi' 'is buttoned breast
As stout as the truth, my sirs! – An' 'is face
As bold as a robin! It's much he cares
For this nice old shame and disgrace.

Oh but he drops his flag when 'e sees me,
Yes, an' 'is face goes white ... oh yes
Tha can stare at me wi' thy fierce blue eyes,
But tha doesna stare me out, I guess!

6

Whativer brings thee out so far
    In a' this depth o' snow?
– I'm takin' 'ome a weddin' dress
    If tha maun know.

Why, is there a weddin' at Underwood,
    As tha ne'd trudge up here?
– It's Widow Naylor's weddin'-dress,
    An' 'er's wantin it, I hear.

46

'*Er* doesna want no weddin-dress . . .
    What – but what dost mean?
– Doesn't ter know what I mean, Tim? – Yi,
    Tha must 'a' been hard to wean!

Tha'rt a good-un at suckin-in yet, Timmy;
    But tell me, isn't it true
As 'er'll be wantin' *my* weddin' dress
    In a week or two?

Tha's no occasions ter ha'e me on
    Lizzie – what's done is done!
– *Done*, I should think so – Done! But might
    I ask when tha begun?

It's thee as 'as done it as much as me,
    Lizzie, I tell thee that.
– 'Me gotten a childt to thy landlady –!'
    Tha's gotten thy answer pat,

As tha allers hast – but let me tell thee
    Hasna ter sent me whoam, when I
Was a'most burstin' mad o' my-sen
    An' walkin' in agony;

After thy kisses, Lizzie, after
    Tha's lain right up to me Lizzie, an' melted
Into me, melted into me, Lizzie,
    Till I was verily swelted.

An' if my landlady seed me like it,
    An' if 'er clawkin', tiger's eyes
Went through me just as the light went out
    Is it any cause for surprise?

No cause for surprise at all, my lad,
    After lickin' and snuffin' at me, tha could
Turn thy mouth on a woman like her –
    Did ter find her good?

Ay, I did, but afterwards
    I should like to ha' killed her!
– Afterwards! – an' after how long
    Wor it tha'd liked to 'a killed her?

Say no more, Liz, dunna thee,
    'I might lose my-sen.
– I'll only say good-bye to thee, Timothy,
    An' gi'e her thee back again.

I'll ta'e thy word 'Good-bye,' Liz,
    But I shonna marry her,
I shonna for nobody. – It is
    Very nice on you, Sir.

The childt maun ta'e its luck, it maun,
    An' she maun ta'e *her* luck,
For I tell ye I shonna marry her –
    What her's got, her took.

That's spoken like a man, Timmy,
    That's spoken like a man . . .
'He up an' fired off his pistol
    An' then away he ran.'

I damn well shanna marry 'er,
    So chew at it no more,
Or I'll chuck the flamin' lot of you –
    – You nedn't have swore.

7

That's his collar round the candle-stick
An' that's the dark blue tie I bought 'im,
An' these is the woman's kids he's so fond on,
An' 'ere comes the cat that caught 'im.

I dunno where his eyes was – a gret
Round-shouldered hag! My sirs, to think
Of him stoopin' to her! You'd wonder he could
Throw hisself in that sink.

I expect you know who I am, Mrs Naylor!
    – Who yer are? – yis, you're Lizzie Stainwright.
'An 'appen you might guess what I've come for?
    – 'Appen I mightn't, 'appen I might.

You knowed as I was courtin' Tim Merfin.
    – Yis, I knowed 'e wor courtin' thee.
An' yet you've been carryin' on wi' him.
    – Ay, an' 'im wi' me.

Well, now you've got to pay for it,
    – An' if I han, what's that to thee?
For 'e isn't goin' to marry you.
    – Is it a toss-up 'twixt thee an' me?

It's no toss-up 'twixt thee an' me.
    – Then what art colleyfoglin' for?
I'm not havin' your orts an' slarts.
    – Which on us said you wor?

I want you to know 'e's non *marryin'* you.
    – Tha wants 'im thy-sen too bad.
Though I'll see as 'e pays you, an' comes to the scratch.
    – Tha'rt for doin' a lot wi' th' lad.

8

To think I should ha'e to haffle an' caffle
  Wi' a woman, an' pay 'er a price
For lettin' me marry the lad as I thought
  To marry wi' cabs an' rice.

But we'll go unbeknown to the registrar,
  An' give *'er* what money there is,
For I won't be beholden to such as her
  For anythink of his.

9

Take off thy duty stripes, Tim,
  An' come wi' me in here,
Ta'e off thy p'lice-man's helmet
  An' look me clear.

I wish tha hadna done it, Tim,
  I do, an' that I do!
For whenever I look thee i' th' face, I s'll see
  Her face too.

I wish tha could wesh 'er off'n thee,
  For I used to think that thy
Face was the finest thing that iver
  Met my eye . . .

10

Twenty pound o' thy own tha hast, and fifty pound ha'e I,
Thine shall go to pay the woman, an' wi' my bit we'll buy
All as we shall want for furniture when tha leaves this
    place,
An' we'll be married at th' registrar – now lift thy face.

Lift thy face an' look at me, man, up an' look at me:
Sorry I am for this business, an' sorry if I ha'e driven thee
To such a thing: but it's a poor tale, that I'm bound to say,
Before I can ta'e thee I've got a widow of forty-five to pay.

Dunnat thee think but what I love thee – I love thee well,
But 'deed an' I wish as this tale o' thine wor niver my tale
    to tell;

50

Deed an' I wish as I could stood at the altar wi' thee an'
    been proud o' thee,
That I could ha' been first woman to thee, as thou'rt first
    man to me.

But we maun ma'e the best on't – I'll rear thy childt if 'er'll
    yield it to me,
An' then wi' that twenty pound we gi'e 'er I s'd think 'er
    wunna be
So very much worser off than 'er wor before – An' now
    look up
An' answer me – for I've said my say, an' there's no more
    sorrow to sup.

Yi, tha'rt a man, tha'rt a fine big man, but niver a baby had
    eyes
As sulky an' ormin' as thine. Hast owt to say otherwise
From what I've arranged wi' thee? Eh man, what a stub-
    born jackass thou art,
Kiss me then – there! – ne'er mind if I scraight – I wor
    fond o' thee, Sweetheart.

THE DRAINED CUP

The snow is witherin' off'n th' gress
    Love, should I tell thee summat?
The snow is witherin' off'n th' gress
An' a thick mist sucks at the clots o' snow,
An' the moon above in a weddin' dress
Goes fogged an' slow –
    Love, should I tell thee summat?

Tha's been snowed up i' this cottage wi' me,
    Nay, I'm tellin' thee summat. –
Tha's bin snowed up i' this cottage wi' me
While th' clocks has a' run down an' stopped

An' the short days withering silently
Unbeknown have dropped.
    – Yea, but I'm tellin' thee summat.

How many days dost think has gone? –
    Now I'm tellin' thee summat.
How many days dost think has gone?
How many days has the candle-light shone
On us as tha got more white an' wan?
– Seven days, or none –
    Am I not tellin' thee summat?

Tha come to bid farewell to me –
    Tha'rt frit o' summat.
To kiss me and shed a tear wi' me,
Then off and away wi' the weddin' ring
For the girl who was grander, and better than me
For marrying –
    Tha'rt frit o' summat?

I durstna kiss thee tha trembles so,
    Tha'rt frit o' summat.
Tha arena very flig to go,
'Appen the mist from the thawin' snow
Daunts thee – it isna for love, I know,
That tha'rt loath to go.
    – Dear o' me, say summat.

Maun tha cling to the wa' as tha goes,
    So bad as that?
Tha'lt niver get into thy weddin' clothes
At that rate – eh, theer goes thy hat;
Ne'er mind, good-bye lad, now I lose
My joy, God knows,
    – An' worse nor that.

The road goes under the apple tree;
    Look, for I'm showin' thee summat.

An' if it worn't for the mist, tha'd see
The great black wood on all sides o' thee
Wi' the little pads going cunningly
To ravel thee.
  So listen, I'm tellin' thee summat.

When tha comes to the beechen avenue,
  I'm warnin' thee o' summat.
Mind tha shall keep inwards, a few
Steps to the right, for the gravel pits
Are steep an' deep wi' watter, an' you
Are scarce o' your wits.
  Remember, I've warned thee o' summat.

An' mind when crossin' the planken bridge,
  Again I warn ye o' summat.
Ye slip not on the slippery ridge
Of the thawin' snow, or it'll be
A long put-back to your gran' marridge,
I'm tellin' ye.
  Nay, are ter scared o' summat?

I'n kep the thick black curtains drawn,
  Am I not tellin' thee summat?
Against the knockin' of sevenfold dawn,
An' red-tipped candles from morn to morn
Have dipped an' danced upon thy brawn
Till thou art worn –
  Oh, I have cost thee summat.

Look in the mirror an' see thy-sen,
  – What, I am showin' thee summat.
Wasted an' wan tha sees thy-sen,
An' thy hand that holds the mirror shakes
Till tha drops the glass and tha shudders when
Thy luck breaks.
  Sure, tha'rt afraid o' summat.

Frail thou art, my saucy man,
   – Listen, I'm tellin' thee summat.
Tottering and tired thou art, my man,
Tha came to say good-bye to me,
An' tha's done it so well, that now I can
Part wi' thee.
   – Master, I'm givin' thee summat.

BALLAD OF ANOTHER OPHELIA

OH the green glimmer of apples in the orchard,
Lamps in a wash of rain!
Oh the wet walk of my brown hen through the stackyard,
Oh tears on the window pane!

Nothing now will ripen the bright green apples,
Full of disappointment and of rain,
Brackish they will taste, of tears, when the yellow dapples
Of autumn tell the withered tale again.

All round the yard it is cluck, my brown hen,
Cluck, and the rain-wet wings,
Cluck, my marigold bird, and again
Cluck for your yellow darlings.

For the grey rat found the gold thirteen
Huddled away in the dark:
Flutter for a moment, oh the beast is quick and keen,
Extinct one yellow-fluffy spark.

Once I had a lover bright like running water,
Once his face was laughing like the sky;
Open like the sky looking down in all its laughter
On the buttercups, and the buttercups was I.

What, then, is there hidden in the skirts of all the blossom?
What is peeping from your wings, oh mother hen?

'Tis the sun who asks the question, in a lovely haste for
    wisdom;
What a lovely haste for wisdom is in men!

Yea, but it is cruel when undressed is all the blossom,
And her shift is lying white upon the floor,
That a grey one, like a shadow, like a rat, a thief, a rain-
    storm,
Creeps upon her then and gathers in his store.

Oh the grey garner that is full of half-grown apples,
Oh the golden sparkles laid extinct!
And oh, behind the cloud-sheaves, like yellow autumn
    dapples,
Did you see the wicked sun that winked!

UNDER THE OAK

You, if you were sensible,
When I tell you the stars flash signals, each one dreadful,
You would not turn and answer me
'The night is wonderful.'

Even you, if you knew
How this darkness soaks me through and through, and
    infuses
Unholy fear in my vapour, you would pause to distinguish
What hurts, from what amuses.

For I tell you
Beneath this powerful tree, my whole soul's fluid
Oozes away from me as a sacrifice steam
At the knife of a Druid.

Again I tell you, I bleed, I am bound with withies,
My life runs out.
I tell you my blood runs out on the floor of this oak,
Gout upon gout.

Above me springs the blood-born mistletoe
In the shady smoke.
But who are you, twittering to and fro
Beneath the oak?

What thing better are you, what worse?
What have you to do with the mysteries
Of this ancient place, of my ancient curse?
What place have you in my histories?

THE NORTH COUNTRY

In another country, black poplars shake themselves over a
    pond,
And rooks and the rising smoke-waves scatter and wheel
    from the works beyond;
The air is dark with north and with sulphur, the grass is a
    darker green,
And people darkly invested with purple move palpable
    through the scene.

Soundlessly down across the counties, out of the resonant
    gloom
That wraps the north in stupor and purple travels the deep,
    slow boom
Of the man-life north-imprisoned, shut in the hum of the
    purpled steel
As it spins to sleep on its motion, drugged dense in the
    sleep of the wheel.

Out of the sleep, from the gloom of motion, soundlessly,
    somnambule
Moans and booms the soul of a people imprisoned, asleep
    in the rule
Of the strong machine that runs mesmeric, booming the
    spell of its word

Upon them and moving them helpless, mechanic, their will
    to its will deferred.

Yet all the while comes the droning inaudible, out of the
    violet air,
The moaning of sleep-bound beings in travail that toil and
    are will-less there
In the spell-bound north, convulsive now with a dream
    near morning, strong
With violent achings heaving to burst the sleep that is now
    not long.

BLUE

THE earth again like a ship steams out of the dark sea over
The edge of the blue, and the sun stands up to see us glide
Slowly into another day; slowly the rover
Vessel of darkness takes the rising tide.

I, on the deck, am startled by this dawn confronting
Me who am issued amazed from the darkness, stripped
And quailing here in the sunshine, betrayed from haunting
The soundless night whereon our days are shipped.

Feeling myself undawning, the day's light playing upon me,
I who am substance of shadow, I all compact
Of the stuff of the night, finding myself all wrongly
Among the crowds of things in the sunshine jostled and
    racked.

I with the night on my lips, I sigh with the silence of death;
And what do I care though the very stones should cry me
    unreal, though the clouds
Shine in conceit of substance upon me, who am less than
    the rain.
Do I not know the darkness within them? What are they
    but shrouds?

The clouds go down the sky with a wealthy ease
Casting a shadow of scorn upon me for my share in death;
but I
Hold my own in the midst of them, darkling, defy
The whole of the day to extinguish the shadow I lift on the
breeze.

Yea, though the very clouds have vantage over me,
Enjoying their glancing flight, though love is dead,
I still am not homeless here, I've a tent by day
Of darkness where she sleeps on her perfect bed.

And I know the Host, the minute sparkling of darkness
Which vibrates untouched and perfect through the gran-
deur of night,
But which, when dawn crows challenge, assaulting the
vivid motes
Of living darkness, bursts fretfully, and is bright:

> Runs like a fretted arc-lamp into light,
> Stirred by conflict to shining, which else
> Were dark and whole with the night.

Runs to a fret of speed like a racing wheel,
Which else were aslumber along with the whole
Of the dark, swinging rhythmic instead of a-reel.

Is chafed to anger, bursts into rage like thunder;
Which else were a silent grasp that held the heavens
Arrested, beating thick with wonder.

Leaps like a fountain of blue sparks leaping
In a jet from out of obscurity,
Which erst was darkness sleeping.

Runs into streams of bright blue drops,
Water and stones and stars, and myriads
Of twin-blue eyes, and crops

Of floury grain, and all the hosts of day,
All lovely hosts of ripples caused by fretting
The Darkness into play.

THE MYSTIC BLUE

OUT of the darkness, fretted sometimes in its sleeping,
Jets of sparks in fountains of blue come leaping
To sight, revealing a secret, numberless secrets keeping.

Sometimes the darkness trapped within a wheel
Runs into speed like a dream, the blue of the steel
Showing the rocking darkness now a-reel.

And out of the invisible, streams of bright blue drops
Rain from the showery heavens, and bright blue crops
Surge from the under-dark to their ladder-tops.

And all the manifold blue and joyous eyes,
The rainbow arching over in the skies,
New sparks of wonder opening in surprise

All these pure things come foam and spray of the sea
Of Darkness abundant, which shaken mysteriously,
Breaks into dazzle of living, as dolphins leap from the sea
Of midnight and shake it to fire, till the flame of the shadow
        we see.

THE CHIEF MYSTERY

THE stinging nettles on my wrists woke me,
        Who had not slept . . .
I do not know where I had been
Nor what had become of me
        But I had not slept . . .
I only know that like a sod
In a meadow lost I lay,

And that a peewit called . . .
> But whether it called in my soul,
> Or whether it rang in the air,
> Or whether my heart was its nest,
> I do not know.

I was there, that was all . . .
And like a sod in a meadow
I was embedded in the rest of things
Along with the moon.
> For the full moon shone; but whether
> It lay on me as on water,
> Or whether I was the darkness with arched wings
> Hovering over it
> To fold in a shining concave the pale night,
> I do not know.

I awoke with the young nettles on my wrists,
> And I lifted my head;

And then I knew I had taken my mouth from her throat –
> And I raised my breast;

Knowing then I had taken my bosom from her crushed
  breasts.
> And I went back with my mouth to her mouth
> So glad to have been lost,
> So glad to find myself again.

Yet looking again at the night
Still I could not distinguish myself:
I said 'This is grass that twinkles in the dark,
> There is something about that they call the wind,
> And that white scud of heaven
> Is a track of clouds across the moon;
> But I, where among them all am I?'

> Then the stinging nettles on my wrists
> Showed me some other lovers stealing down the other
>   hedgerow,

And I lay close down,
Saying 'It is she – it is I –
That is her small ear against my eyes,
This is I – this is I –

Perhaps the tiny young nettles have stung her ears.'
And I took her ear like the leaf of a water-flower between
     my lips,
And I said 'Love?'
For I was not sure of myself.
But she put her fingers on my neck, under my collar,
And her fingers were cool,
And I said, ''Tis I,
I am here!'

'Look! We Have Come Through!'

BALLAD OF A WILFUL WOMAN

First Part

Upon her plodding palfrey
With a heavy child at her breast
And Joseph holding the bridle
They mount to the last hill-crest.

Dissatisfied and weary
She sees the blade of the sea
Dividing earth and heaven
In a glitter of ecstasy.

Sudden a dark-faced stranger
With his back to the sun, holds out
His arms; so she lights from her palfrey
And turns her round about.

She has given the child to Joseph,
Gone down to the flashing shore;
And Joseph, shading his eyes with his hand,
Stands watching evermore.

Second Part

The sea in the stones is singing,
A woman binds her hair
With yellow, frail sea-poppies,
That shine as her fingers stir.

While a naked man comes swiftly
Like a spurt of white foam rent
From the crest of a falling breaker,
Over the poppies sent.

He puts his surf-wet fingers
Over her startled eyes,
And asks if she sees the land, the land,
The land of her glad surmise.

Third Part

AGAIN in her blue, blue mantle
Riding at Joseph's side,
She says, 'I went to Cythera,
And woe betide!'

Her heart is a swinging cradle
That holds the perfect child,
But the shade on her forehead ill becomes
A mother mild.

So on with the slow, mean journey
In the pride of humility;
Till they halt at a cliff on the edge of the land
Over a sullen sea.

While Joseph pitches the sleep-tent
She goes far down to the shore
To where a man in a heaving boat
Waits with a lifted oar.

Fourth Part

THEY dwelt in a huge, hoarse sea-cave
And looked far down the dark
Where an archway torn and glittering
Shone like a huge sea-spark.

He said: 'Do you see the spirits
Crowding the bright doorway?'
He said: 'Do you hear them whispering?'
He said: 'Do you catch what they say?'

Fifth Part

THEN Joseph, grey with waiting,
His dark eyes full of pain,
Heard: 'I have been to Patmos;
Give me the child again.'

Now on with the hopeless journey
Looking bleak ahead she rode,
And the man and the child of no more account
Than the earth the palfrey trode.

Till a beggar spoke to Joseph,
But looked into her eyes;
So she turned, and said to her husband:
'I give, whoever denies.'

Sixth Part

SHE gave on the open heather
Beneath bare judgment stars,
And she dreamed of her children and Joseph,
And the isles, and her men, and her scars.

And she woke to distil the berries
The beggar had gathered at night,
Whence he drew the curious liquors
He held in delight.

He gave her no crown of flowers,
No child and no palfrey slow,
Only led her through harsh, hard places
Where strange winds blow.

She follows his restless wanderings
Till night when, by the fire's red stain,
Her face is bent in the bitter steam
That comes from the flowers of pain.

Then merciless and ruthless
He takes the flame-wild drops
To the town, and tries to sell them
With the market-crops.

So she follows the cruel journey
That ends not anywhere,
And dreams, as she stirs the mixing-pot,
She is brewing hope from despair.

TRIER

BEI HENNEF

THE little river twittering in the twilight,
The wan, wandering look of the pale sky,
  This is almost bliss.

And everything shut up and gone to sleep,
All the troubles and anxieties and pain
  Gone under the twilight.

Only the twilight now, and the soft 'Sh!' of the river
  That will last for ever.

And at last I know my love for you is here;
I can see it all, it is whole like the twilight,
It is large, so large, I could not see it before,
Because of the little lights and flickers and interruptions,
  Troubles, anxieties and pains.

You are the call and I am the answer,
You are the wish, and I the fulfilment,
You are the night, and I the day.
  What else? it is perfect enough.
  It is perfectly complete,
  You and I,
  What more –?

Strange, how we suffer in spite of this!

HENNEF AM RHEIN

FIRST MORNING

THE night was a failure
  but why not –?

In the darkness
  with the pale dawn seething at the window
  through the black frame
  I could not be free,
  not free myself from the past, those others –
  and our love was a confusion,
  there was a horror,
  you recoiled away from me.

Now, in the morning
As we sit in the sunshine on the seat by the little shrine,
And look at the mountain-walls,
Walls of blue shadow,
And see so near at our feet in the meadow
Myriads of dandelion pappus
Bubbles ravelled in the dark green grass
Held still beneath the sunshine –
It is enough, you are near –
The mountains are balanced,
The dandelion seeds stay half-submerged in the grass;
You and I together
We hold them proud and blithe
On our love.
They stand upright on our love,
Everything starts from us,
We are the source.

BEUERBERG

MUTILATION

A THICK mist-sheet lies over the broken wheat.
I walk up to my neck in mist, holding my mouth up.
Across there, a discoloured moon burns itself out.

I hold the night in horror;
I dare not turn round.

To-night I have left her alone.
They would have it I have left her for ever.

Oh my God, how it aches
Where she is cut off from me!

Perhaps she will go back to England.
Perhaps she will go back,
Perhaps we are parted for ever.

If I go on walking through the whole breadth of Germany
I come to the North Sea, or the Baltic.

Over there is Russia – Austria, Switzerland, France, in a
circle!
I here in the undermist on the Bavarian road.

It aches in me.
What is England or France, far off,
But a name she might take?
I don't mind this continent stretching, the sea far away;
It aches in me for her
Like the agony of limbs cut off and aching;
Not even longing,
It is only agony.

A cripple!
Oh God, to be mutilated!
To be a cripple!

And if I never see her again?

I think, if they told me so
I could convulse the heavens with my horror.
I think I could alter the frame of things in my agony.
I think I could break the System with my heart.
I think, in my convulsion, the skies would break.

She too suffers.
But who could compel her, if she chose me against them
    all?
She has not chosen me finally, she suspends her choice.
Night folk, Tuatha De Danaan, dark Gods, govern her
    sleep,
Magnificent ghosts of the darkness, carry off her decision
    in sleep,
Leave her no choice, make her lapse me-ward, make her,
Oh Gods of the living Darkness, powers of Night.

WOLFRATSHAUSEN

GREEN

THE dawn was apple-green,
    The sky was green wine held up in the sun,
The moon was a golden petal between.

She opened her eyes, and green
    They shone, clear like flowers undone
For the first time, now for the first time seen.

ICKING

RIVER ROSES

BY the Isar, in the twilight
We were wandering and singing,
By the Isar, in the evening
We climbed the huntsman's ladder and sat swinging

71

In the fir-tree overlooking the marshes,
While river met with river, and the ringing
Of their pale-green glacier-water filled the evening.

By the Isar, in the twilight
We found the dark wild roses
Hanging red at the river; and simmering
Frogs were singing, and over the river closes
Was savour of ice and of roses; and glimmering
Fear was abroad. We whispered: 'No one knows us.
Let it be as the snake disposes
Here in this simmering marsh.'

KLOSTER SCHAEFTLARN

GLOIRE DE DIJON

WHEN she rises in the morning
I linger to watch her;
She spreads the bath-cloth underneath the window
And the sunbeams catch her
Glistening white on the shoulders,
While down her sides the mellow
Golden shadow glows as
She stoops to the sponge, and her swung breasts
Sway like full-blown yellow
Gloire de Dijon roses.

She drips herself with water, and her shoulders
Glisten as silver, they crumple up
Like wet and falling roses, and I listen
For the sluicing of their rain-dishevelled petals.
In the window full of sunlight
Concentrates her golden shadow
Fold on fold, until it glows as
Mellow as the glory roses.

ICKING

A DOE AT EVENING

As I went through the marshes
a doe sprang out of the corn
and flashed up the hill-side
leaving her fawn.

On the sky-line
she moved round to watch,
she pricked a fine black blotch
on the sky.

I looked at her
and felt her watching;
I became a strange being.
Still, I had my right to be there with her.

Her nimble shadow trotting
along the sky-line, she
put back her fine, level-balanced head.
And I knew her.

Ah yes, being male, is not my head hard-balanced, antlered?
Are not my haunches light?
Has she not fled on the same wind with me?
Does not my fear cover her fear?

IRSCHENHAUSEN

MISERY

OUT of this oubliette between the mountains
five valleys go, five passes like gates;
three of them black in shadow, two of them bright
with distant sunshine;
and sunshine fills one high valley bed,
green grass shining, and little white houses
like quartz crystals,
little, but distinct a way off.

Why don't I go?
Why do I crawl about this pot, this oubliette, stupidly?
Why don't I go?

But where?
If I come to a pine-wood, I can't say
Now I am arrived!
What are so many straight trees to me!

STERZING

MEETING AMONG THE MOUNTAINS

THE little pansies by the road have turned
Away their purple faces and their gold;
And evening has taken all the bees from the wild thyme
And all the scent is shed away by the cold.

Against the hard pale-blue evening sky
The mountains' new-dropped summer snow is clear
Glistening in steadfast stillness-clear
Like clean pain sending on us a chill down here.

Christ on the cross, his beautiful young man's body
Has fallen forward on the nails, and hangs
White and loose at last, with all his pain
Drawn on his mouth, eyes broken in the final pangs.

And slowly down the mountain road, a belated
Bullock wagon comes: Lo I am ashamed
To gaze any more at the Christ, whom the mountain snows
Whitely confront, my heart shrinks back, inflamed.

The breath of the bullock steams on the hard chill air;
The band across its brow, it scarcely seems
To draw the load, so slow and dull it moves
While the driver sits on the left-hand shaft and dreams.

Surely about his sunbrowned handsome face, something
That vexes me with memory! He sits so still
Here among all this silence, crouching forward
Dreaming and letting the bullock take its will.

I stand aside on the grass to let them go,
And, Christ, again have I met his eyes, again
The brown eyes black with misery and hate, that look
Full into mine, and the torment starts again.

One moment the hate leaps at me standing there,
One moment I see the stillness of agony
Something frozen in silence, that dare not be
Loosed; one moment the darkness frightens me.

Then among the averted pansies, below the high
White peaks of snow, at the foot of the sunken Christ,
I stood in a chill of anguish trying to say
The joy I bought was not too highly priced.

But he was gone, motionless, hating me,
Enduring as the mountains do, because they are strong,
But a pale dead Christ on the crucifix of his heart
And breathing the frozen memory of his wrong.

Still in his nostrils the frozen breath of despair,
And in his heart the half-numbed agony;
In his clenched fist the shame and in
His belly the smouldering hate of me.

And I, as I stand in the cold averted flowers,
Feel the shame that clenches his fists like nails through my
    own,
Feel the despair on his brow like a crown of thorns
And his frozen anguish turning my heart to stone.

TUXTAL

GIORNO DEI MORTI

ALONG the avenue of cypresses
All in their scarlet cloaks, and surplices
Of linen go the chanting choristers,
The priests in gold and black, the villagers . . .

And all along the path to the cemetery
The round dark heads of men crowd silently,
And black-scarved faces of women-folk, wistfully
Watch at the banner of death, and the mystery.

And at the foot of a grave a father stands
With sunken head, and forgotten, folded hands;
And at the foot of a grave a mother kneels
With pale shut face, nor either hears nor feels

The coming of the chanting choristers
Between the avenue of cypresses,
The silence of the many villagers,
The candle-flames beside the surplices.

THE YOUNG SOLDIER WITH BLOODY SPURS

A Servant Girl Speaks

THE sergeant says that eight and twenty wagons
Are coming behind, and we must put out all
The water we can at the gate, for the horses. He gallops
To the next farm, pulls up where the elder flowers fall.

The wheat on both sides of the road stands green,
And hundreds of soldiers on horseback have filed between
It, gone by our farm to the mountains that stand back blue
This morning.

　　　I think perhaps the man that came
To Wolfrathausen last winter's end, comes through

76

This place to-day. These soldiers wear the same
Helmets as his he lost in the wood that night,
And their uniforms are the same of white and blue –

It was cold, and he put his cloak right round me
As we walked; dark, so he held his arm close round me.
In the stillness, he took off his helmet to kiss me –
It snowed, and his helmet was lost, he forgot me, he did
    not miss me.

The Isar whispers again in the valley; the children
Are ducking their heads in the water tubs at the gate
As they go from school; some of the officers rally
At the door of the Gasthaus down the road: great
Threads of blue wind far and down the road
I wait for the eight and twenty wagons to come.

At last I hear a rattle, and there away
Crawls the first load into sight – and now there are some
Drawing near, they cover the München road.
                     Nay
I dread him coming; I wonder how he will take it.
I can see his raging black eyes blaze at me
And feel him gripping my wrist as if he would break it.

Here comes the first of the wagons, a grey, a dreary
Shut-up coffin of a thing, with a soldier weary
In the box, and four hot horses going drearily,
And a soldier in the saddle of the left-hand draught-horse,
    sitting wearily.

One by one they go by – at last
There he sits in the saddle of this the five
And twentieth wagon. And he will not drive past
He pulls up for our water; would he drive
On if he knew that *I* was at this farm?

And he swings his heavy thigh
Out of the saddle, and staggering

With stiffness comes for the water that I
Have poured for the horses – a dark-blue, staggering
Strong young man. He leans sighing
With head against the shaft, and takes
His helmet off, and wipes his hair, trying
To ease himself in his clothes. It makes
Me want to cry, to see him so strong and easy
Swarthy and strong with his damp thick hair
Pushed up on end – and the breath sighing
Between his thick lips. I wonder where
He thinks I am – if ever he thinks at all.
But his handkerchief is white with a broad blue border,
A nice one, I like it. He'll think it's a tall order
When I say he ought to marry me. And small
I feel I have to tell him.

                     But why, before
He waters the horses does he wash his heel?
Jesus! – his spurs are red with shining blood!
He splashes water from the pail upon them,
And rubs the silver clean with his thick brown fingers,
Bending backwards awkwardly,
And anxiously, like a boy afraid to be found out.

And he goes and washes the belly of his horse,
A poor roan thing: its hind leg twitches
Forwards as he rubs the wound,
And bloody water falls upon the road
Soiling the clean white dust. He rubs the belly
Carefully again, and again, to stop the bleeding.
Jesus! – his fingers are red!
And again, rolling in his heavy high boots,
He comes to the side of the road and washes his hand,
And looks round again at his heel, the bright spur,
And bends again and looks at the belly of the horse,
And kicks dust over the red stain in the road.

And all the time his handsome, swarthy red face
With savage black eyes is sulky: and all the time
He frowns as if he were worried, as if the place
On the horse's belly hurt him, for he was rather gentle
To the thing, and rather fretted. And his thick black hair
Was wet with sweat, and his movements strong and heavy.
– I wonder, will he care!

Now I take the big stone jug of water
Down to the gate, and stand and wait
For a word. He is coming towards the gate –
His eyes meet mine as he takes the jug of water,
He knows me, but does not speak: instead
He drinks and drinks, then turns away his head.

'Do you remember me?'
– 'Yes!'
'Who then?'
– 'Maria, of the Gasthaus Green Hat, Wolfrathausen.'
'I am with child by you –'
He looked at me, and his heavy brows came over
His eyes and he sulked. He had another lover.

'It is true,' I said.
– 'And what do you want?'
'What do you think?' I said.

He looked away down the road

Suddenly his horses began to start.
He shouted, ran heavily after them,
And jerked back their bridles, pushing their heads apart
I waited, but he would not come back to me,
He stayed with the horses, sulkily,
Till the whistle went. Then swiftly he

Swung strong and heavy to saddle again
And called to his horses, and his strong blue body

79

Had its back to me;
And away went the last of the wagons.

NEW YEAR'S NIGHT

Now you are mine, to-night at last I say it;
You're a dove I have bought for sacrifice,
And to-night I slay it.

Here in my arms my naked sacrifice!
Death, do you hear, in my arms I am bringing
My offering, bought at great price.

She's a silvery dove worth more than all I've got.
Now I offer her up to the ancient, inexorable God,
Who knows me not.

Look, she's a wonderful dove, without blemish or spot!
I sacrifice all in her, my last of the world,
Pride, strength, all the lot.

All, all on the altar! And death swooping down
Like a falcon. 'Tis God has taken the victim;
I have won my renown.

RABBIT SNARED IN THE NIGHT

Why do you spurt and sprottle
like that, bunny?
Why should I want to throttle
you, bunny?

Yes, bunch yourself between
my knees and lie still.
Lie on me with a hot, plumb, live weight,
heavy as a stone, passive,
yet hot, waiting.

What are you waiting for?
What are you waiting for?
What is the hot, plumb weight of your desire on me?
You have a hot, unthinkable desire of me, bunny.

What is that spark
glittering at me on the unutterable darkness
of your eye, bunny?
The finest splinter of a spark
that you throw off, straight on the tinder of my nerves!

It sets up a strange fire,
a soft, most unwarrantable burning
a bale-fire mounting, mounting up in me.

'Tis not of me, bunny.
It was you engendered it,
with that fine, demoniacal spark
you jetted off your eye at me.

I did not want it,
this furnace, this draught-maddened fire
which mounts up my arms
making them swell with turgid, ungovernable strength.

'Twas not *I* that wished it,
that my fingers should turn into these flames
avid and terrible
that they are at this moment.

It must have been *your* inbreathing, gaping desire
that drew this red gush in me;
I must be reciprocating *your* vacuous, hideous passion.

It must be the want in you
that has drawn this terrible draught of white fire
up my veins as up a chimney.

It must be you who desire
this intermingling of the black and monstrous fingers of
    Moloch
in the blood-jets of your throat.

Come, you shall have your desire,
since already I am implicated with you
in your strange lust.

PARADISE RE-ENTERED

THROUGH the strait gate of passion,
Between the bickering fire
Where flames of fierce love tremble
On the body of fierce desire:

To the intoxication,
The mind, fused down like a bead,
Flees in its agitation
The flames' stiff speed:

At last to calm incandescence,
Burned clean by remorseless hate,
Now, at the day's renascence
We approach the gate.

Now, from the darkened spaces
Of fear, and of frightened faces,
Death, in our awful embraces
Approached and passed by;

We near the flame-burnt porches
Where the brands of the angels, like torches
Whirl, – in these perilous marches
Pausing to sigh;

We look back on the withering roses,
The stars, in their sun-dimmed closes,

Where 'twas given us to repose us
Sure on our sanctity;

Beautiful, candid lovers,
Burnt out of our earthy covers,
We might have nestled like plovers
In the fields of eternity.

There, sure in sinless being,
All-seen, and then all-seeing,
In us life unto death agreeing,
We might have lain.

But we storm the angel-guarded
Gates of the long-discarded
Garden, which God has hoarded
Against our pain.

The Lord of Hosts, and the Devil
Are left on Eternity's level
Field, and as victors we travel
To Eden home.

Back beyond good and evil
Return we. Eve dishevel
Your hair for the bliss-drenched revel
On our primal loam.

SONG OF A MAN WHO HAS COME THROUGH

Not I, not I, but the wind that blows through me!
A fine wind is blowing the new direction of Time.
If only I let it bear me, carry me, if only it carry me!
If only I am sensitive, subtle, oh, delicate, a winged gift!
If only, most lovely of all, I yield myself and am borrowed
By the fine, fine wind that takes its course through the
    chaos of the world

Like a fine, an exquisite chisel, a wedge-blade inserted;
If only I am keen and hard like the sheer tip of a wedge
Driven by invisible blows,
The rock will split, we shall come at the wonder, we shall
    find the Hesperides.

Oh, for the wonder that bubbles into my soul,
I would be a good fountain, a good well-head,
Would blur no whisper, spoil no expression.

What is the knocking?
What is the knocking at the door in the night?
It is somebody wants to do us harm.

No, no, it is the three strange angels.
Admit them, admit them.

'SHE SAID AS WELL TO ME'

SHE said as well to me: 'Why are you ashamed?
That little bit of your chest that shows between
the gap of your shirt, why cover it up?
Why shouldn't your legs and your good strong thighs
be rough and hairy? – I'm glad they are like that.
You are shy, you silly, you silly shy thing.
Men are the shyest creatures, they never will come
out of their covers. Like any snake
slipping into its bed of dead leaves, you hurry into your
    clothes.
And I love you so! Straight and clean and all of a piece is
    the body of a man,
such an instrument, a spade, like a spear, or an oar,
such a joy to me –'
So she laid her hands and pressed them down my sides,
so that I began to wonder over myself, and what I was.

She said to me: 'What an instrument, your body!
single and perfectly distinct from everything else!
What a tool in the hands of the Lord!
Only God could have brought it to its shape.
It feels as if his handgrasp, wearing you
had polished you and hollowed you,
hollowed this groove in your sides, grasped you under the
    breasts
and brought you to the very quick of your form,
subtler than an old, soft-worn fiddle-bow.

'When I was a child, I loved my father's riding-whip
that he used so often.
I loved to handle it, it seemed like a near part of him.
So I did his pens, and the jasper seal on his desk.
Something seemed to surge through me when I touched
    them.

'So it is with you, but here
The joy I feel!
God knows what I feel, but it is joy!
Look, you are clean and fine and singled out!
I admire you so, you are beautiful: this clean sweep of your
    sides, this firmness, this hard mould!
I would die rather than have it injured with one scar.
I wish I could grip you like the fist of the Lord,
and have you –'

So she said, and I wondered,
feeling trammelled and hurt.
It did not make me free.

Now I say to her: 'No tool, no instrument, no God!
Don't touch me and appreciate me.
It is an infamy.
You would think twice before you touched a weasel on a
    fence

as it lifts its straight white throat.
Your hand would not be so flig and easy.
Nor the adder we saw asleep with her head on her shoulder,
curled up in the sunshine like a princess;
when she lifted her head in delicate, startled wonder
you did not stretch forward to caress her
though she looked rarely beautiful
and a miracle as she glided delicately away, with such
    dignity.
And the young bull in the field, with his wrinkled, sad face,
you are afraid if he rises to his feet,
though he is all wistful and pathetic, like a monolith
    arrested, static.

'Is there nothing in me to make you hesitate?
I tell you there is all these.
And why should you overlook them in me? –'

CRAVING FOR SPRING

I wish it were spring in the world.

Let it be spring!
Come, bubbling, surging tide of sap!
Come, rush of creation!
Come, life! surge through this mass of mortification!
Come, sweep away these exquisite, ghastly first-flowers,
which are rather last-flowers!
Come, thaw down their cool portentousness, dissolve
    them;
snowdrops, straight, death-veined exhalations of white and
    purple crocuses,
flowers of the penumbra, issue of corruption, nourished in
    mortification,
jets of exquisite finality;
Come, spring, make havoc of them!

I trample on the snowdrops, it gives me pleasure to tread
    down the jonquils,
to destroy the chill Lent lilies;
for I am sick of them, their faint-bloodedness,
slow-blooded, icy-fleshed, portentous.

I want the fine, kindling wine-sap of spring,
gold, and of inconceivably fine, quintessential brightness,
rare almost as beams, yet overwhelmingly potent,
strong like the greatest force of world-balancing.

This is the same that picks up the harvest of wheat
and rocks it, tons of grain, on the ripening wind;
the same that dangles the globe-shaped pleiads of fruit
temptingly in mid-air, between a playful thumb and finger;
oh, and suddenly, from out of nowhere, whirls the pear-
    bloom,
upon us, and apple- and almond- and apricot- and quince-
    blossom,
storms and cumulus clouds of all imaginable blossom
about our bewildered faces,
though we do not worship.

I wish it were spring
cunningly blowing on the fallen sparks, odds and ends of
    the old, scattered fire,
and kindling shapely little conflagrations
curious long-legged foals, and wide-eared calves, and
    naked sparrow-bubs.

I wish that spring
would start the thundering traffic of feet
new feet on the earth, beating with impatience.

I wish it were spring, thundering
delicate, tender spring.
I wish these brittle, frost-lovely flowers of passionate,
    mysterious corruption

87

were not yet to come still more from the still-flickering
   discontent.

Oh, in the spring, the bluebell bows him down for very
   exuberance,
exulting with secret warm excess,
bowed down with his inner magnificence!

Oh, yes, the gush of spring is strong enough
to toss the globe of earth like a ball on a water-jet
dancing sportfully;
as you see a tiny celluloid ball tossing on a squirt of water
for men to shoot at, penny-a-time, in a booth at a fair.

The gush of spring is strong enough
to play with the globe of earth like a ball on a fountain;
At the same time it opens the tiny hands of the hazel
with such infinite patience.

The power of the rising, golden, all-creative sap could take
   the earth
and heave it off among the stars, into the invisible;
the same sets the throstle at sunset on a bough
singing against the blackbird;
comes out in the hesitating tremor of the primrose,
and betrays its candour in the round white strawberry
   flower,
is dignified in the foxglove, like a Red-Indian brave.

Ah come, come quickly, spring!
Come and lift us towards our culmination, we myriads;
we who have never flowered, like patient cactuses.
Come and lift us to our end, to blossom, bring us to our
   summer
we who are winter-weary in the winter of the world.
Come making the chaffinch nests hollow and cosy,

come and soften the willow buds till they are puffed and
    furred,
then blow them over with gold.
Come and cajole the gawky colt's-foot flowers.

Come quickly, and vindicate us
against too much death.
Come quickly, and stir the rotten globe of the world from
    within,
burst it with germination, with world anew.
Come now, to us, your adherents, who cannot flower from
    the ice.
All the world gleams with the lilies of Death the Un-
    conquerable,
but come, give us our turn.
Enough of the virgins and lilies, of passionate, suffocating
    perfume of corruption,
no more narcissus perfume, lily harlots, the blades of
    sensation
piercing the flesh to blossom of death.
Have done, have done with this shuddering, delicious
    business
of thrilling ruin in the flesh, of pungent passion, of rare,
    death-edged ecstasy.
Give us our turn, give us a chance, let our hour strike,
O soon, soon!

Let the darkness turn violet with rich dawn.
Let the darkness be warmed, warmed through to a ruddy
    violet,
incipient purpling towards summer in the world of the
    heart of man.

Are the violets already here!
Show me! I tremble so much to hear it, that even now
on the threshold of spring, I fear I shall die.
Show me the violets that are out.

Oh, if it be true, and the living darkness of the blood of
    man is purpling with violets,
if the violets are coming out from under the rack of men,
    winter-rotten and fallen
we shall have spring.
Pray not to die on this Pisgah blossoming with violets.
Pray to live through.

If you catch a whiff of violets from the darkness of the
    shadow of man
it will be spring in the world,
it will be spring in the world of the living;
wonderment organising itself, heralding itself with the
    violets,
stirring of new seasons.

Ah, do not let me die on the brink of such anticipation!
Worse, let me not deceive myself.

                                        ZENNOR

Birds, Beasts and Flowers

FRUITS

POMEGRANATE

You tell me I am wrong.
Who are you, who is anybody to tell me I am wrong?
I am not wrong.

In Syracuse, rock left bare by the viciousness of Greek
      women,
No doubt you have forgotten the pomegranate-trees in
      flower,
Oh so red, and such a lot of them.

Whereas at Venice
Abhorrent, green, slippery city
Whose Doges were old, and had ancient eyes,
In the dense foliage of the inner garden
Pomegranates like bright green stone,
And barbed, barbed with a crown.
Oh, crown of spiked green metal
Actually growing!

Now in Tuscany,
Pomegranates to warm your hands at;
And crowns, kingly, generous, tilting crowns
Over the left eyebrow.

And, if you dare, the fissure!

Do you mean to tell me you will see no fissure?
Do you prefer to look on the plain side?

For all that, the setting suns are open.
The end cracks open with the beginning:
Rosy, tender, glittering within the fissure.

Do you mean to tell me there should be no fissure?
No glittering, compact drops of dawn?
Do you mean it is wrong, the gold-filmed skin, integument,
    shown ruptured?

For my part, I prefer my heart to be broken.
It is so lovely, dawn-kaleidoscopic within the crack.

SAN GERVASIO IN TUSCANY

MEDLARS AND SORB-APPLES

I LOVE you, rotten,
Delicious rottenness.

I love to suck you out from your skins
So brown and soft and coming suave,
So morbid, as the Italians say.

What a rare, powerful, reminiscent flavour
Comes out of your falling through the stages of decay:
Stream within stream.

Something of the same flavour as Syracusan muscat wine
Or vulgar Marsala.

Though even the word Marsala will smack of preciosity
Soon in the pussy-foot West.

What is it?
What is it, in the grape-turning-raisin,
In the medlar, in the sorb-apple,
Wineskins of brown morbidity,
Autumnal excrementa;
What is it that reminds us of white gods?

Gods nude as blanched nut-kernels,
Strangely, half sinisterly flesh-fragrant
As if with sweat,
And drenched with mystery.

Sorb-apples, medlars with dead crowns.

I say, wonderful are the hellish experiences,
Orphic, delicate
Dionysos of the Underworld.

A kiss, and a spasm of farewell, a moment's orgasm of
   rupture
Then along the damp road alone, till the next turning.
And there, a new partner, a new parting, a new unfusing
   into twain,
A new gasp of further isolation,
A new intoxication of loneliness, among decaying, frost-
   cold leaves.

Going down the strange lanes of hell, more and more
   intensely alone,
The fibres of the heart parting one after the other
And yet the soul continuing, naked-footed, ever more
   vividly embodied
Like a flame blown whiter and whiter
In a deeper and deeper darkness
Ever more exquisite, distilled in separation.

So, in the strange retorts of medlars and sorb-apples
The distilled essence of hell.
The exquisite odour of leave-taking.
   Jamque vale!
Orpheus, and the winding, leaf-clogged, silent lanes of hell.

Each soul departing with its own isolation,
Strangest of all strange companions,
And best.

Medlars, sorb-apples
More than sweet
Flux of autumn
Sucked out of your empty bladders

And sipped down, perhaps, with a sip of Marsala
So that the rambling, sky-dropped grape can add its music
    to yours,
Orphic farewell, and farewell, and farewell
And the *ego sum* of Dionysos
The *sono io* of perfect drunkenness
Intoxication of final loneliness.

SAN GERVASIO

FIGS

THE proper way to eat a fig, in society,
Is to split it in four, holding it by the stump,
And open it, so that it is a glittering, rosy, moist, honied,
    heavy-petalled four-petalled flower.

Then you throw away the skin
Which is just like a four-sepalled calyx,
After you have taken off the blossom with your lips.

But the vulgar way
Is just to put your mouth to the crack, and take out the
    flesh in one bite.

Every fruit has its secret.

The fig is a very secretive fruit.
As you see it standing growing, you feel at once it is
    symbolic:
And it seems male.
But when you come to know it better, you agree with the
    Romans, it is female.

The Italians vulgarly say, it stands for the female part; the
    fig-fruit:
The fissure, the yoni,
The wonderful moist conductivity towards the centre.

Involved,
Inturned,
The flowering all inward and womb-fibrilled;
And but one orifice.

The fig, the horse-shoe, the squash-blossom.
Symbols.

There was a flower that flowered inward, womb-ward;
Now there is a fruit like a ripe womb.

It was always a secret.
That's how it should be, the female should always be secret.

There never was any standing aloft and unfolded on a
      bough
Like other flowers, in a revelation of petals;
Silver-pink peach, venetian green glass of medlars and
      sorb-apples,
Shallow wine-cups on short, bulging stems
Openly pledging heaven:
Here's to the thorn in flower! Here is to Utterance!
The brave, adventurous rosaceæ.

Folded upon itself, and secret unutterable,
And milky-sapped, sap that curdles milk and makes *ricotta*,
Sap that smells strange on your fingers, that even goats
      won't taste it;
Folded upon itself, enclosed like any Mohammedan woman,
Its nakedness all within-walls, its flowering forever unseen,
One small way of access only, and this close-curtained from
      the light;
Fig, fruit of the female mystery, covert and inward,
Mediterranean fruit, with your covert nakedness,
Where everything happens invisible, flowering and fertilis-
      ation, and fruiting
In the inwardness of your you, that eye will never see

Till it's finished, and you're over-ripe, and you burst to
    give up your ghost.

Till the drop of ripeness exudes,
And the year is over.

And then the fig has kept her secret long enough.
So it explodes, and you see through the fissure the scarlet.
And the fig is finished, the year is over.

That's how the fig dies, showing her crimson through the
    purple slit
Like a wound, the exposure of her secret, on the open day.
Like a prostitute, the bursten fig, making a show of her
    secret.

That's how women die too.

The year is fallen over-ripe,
The year of our women.
The year of our women is fallen over-ripe.
The secret is laid bare.
And rottenness soon sets in.
The year of our women is fallen over-ripe.

When Eve once knew *in her mind* that she was naked
She quickly sewed fig-leaves, and sewed the same for the
    man.
She'd been naked all her days before,
But till then, till that apple of knowledge, she hadn't had
    the fact on her mind.

She got the fact on her mind, and quickly sewed fig-leaves.
And women have been sewing ever since.
But now they stitch to adorn the bursten fig, not to cover it.
They have their nakedness more than ever on their mind,
And they won't let us forget it.

Now, the secret
Becomes an affirmation through moist, scarlet lips
That laugh at the Lord's indignation.

What then, good Lord! cry the women.
We have kept our secret long enough.
We are a ripe fig.
Let us burst into affirmation.

They forget, ripe figs won't keep.
Ripe figs won't keep.

Honey-white figs of the north, black figs with scarlet inside,
    of the south.
Ripe figs won't keep, won't keep in any clime.
What then, when women the world over have all bursten
    into affirmation?
And bursten figs won't keep?

SAN GERVASIO

GRAPES

So many fruits come from roses
From the rose of all roses
From the unfolded rose
Rose of all the world.

Admit that apples and strawberries and peaches and pears
    and blackberries
Are all Rosaceæ,
Issue of the explicit rose,
The open-countenanced, skyward-smiling rose.

What then of the vine?
Oh, what of the tendrilled vine?

Ours is the universe of the unfolded rose,
The explicit
The candid revelation.

But long ago, oh, long ago
Before the rose began to simper supreme,
Before the rose of all roses, rose of all the world, was even
    in bud,
Before the glaciers were gathered up in a bunch out of the
    unsettled seas and winds,
Or else before they had been let down again, in Noah's
    flood,
There was another world, a dusky, flowerless, tendrilled
    world
And creatures webbed and marshy,
And on the margin, men soft-footed and pristine,
Still, and sensitive, and active,
Audile, tactile sensitiveness as of a tendril which orientates
    and reaches out,
Reaching out and grasping by an instinct more delicate than
    the moon's as she feels for the tides.

Of which world, the vine was the invisible rose,
Before petals spread, before colour made its disturbance,
    before eyes saw too much.

In a green, muddy, web-foot, unutterably songless world
The vine was rose of all roses.

There were no poppies or carnations,
Hardly a greenish lily, watery faint.
Green, dim, invisible flourishing of vines
Royally gesticulate.

Look now even now, how it keeps its power of invisibility!
Look how black, how blue-black, how globed in Egyptian
    darkness
Dropping among his leaves, hangs the dark grape!
See him there, the swart, so palpably invisible:
Whom shall we ask about him?

The negro might know a little.
When the vine was rose, Gods were dark-skinned.
Bacchus is a dream's dream.
Once God was all negroid, as now he is fair.
But it's so long ago, the ancient Bushman has forgotten
    more utterly than we, who have never known.

For we are on the brink of re-remembrance.
Which, I suppose, is why America has gone dry.
Our pale day is sinking into twilight,
And if we sip the wine, we find dreams coming upon us
Out of the imminent night.
Nay, we find ourselves crossing the fern-scented frontiers
Of the world before the floods, where man was dark and
    evasive
And the tiny vine-flower rose of all roses, perfumed,
And all in naked communion communicating as now our
    clothed vision can never communicate.
Vistas, down dark avenues
As we sip the wine.

The grape is swart, the avenues dusky and tendrilled,
    subtly prehensile,
But we, as we start awake, clutch at our vistas democratic,
    boulevards, tram-cars, policemen.
Give us our own back,
Let us go to the soda-fountain, to get sober.

Soberness, sobriety.
It is like the agonised perverseness of a child heavy with
    sleep, yet fighting, fighting to keep awake;
Soberness, sobriety, with heavy eyes propped open.

Dusky are the avenues of wine,
And we must cross the frontiers, though we will not,
Of the lost, fern-scented world:

Take the fern-seed on our lips,
Close the eyes, and go
Down the tendrilled avenues of wine and the otherworld.

SAN GERVASIO

TREES

CYPRESSES

TUSCAN cypresses,
What is it?

Folded in like a dark thought
For which the language is lost,
Tuscan cypresses,
Is there a great secret?
Are our words no good?

The undeliverable secret,
Dead with a dead race and a dead speech, and yet
Darkly monumental in you,
Etruscan cypresses.

Ah, how I admire your fidelity,
Dark cypresses!

Is it the secret of the long-nosed Etruscans?
The long-nosed, sensitive-footed, subtly-smiling Etrus-
cans,
Who made so little noise outside the cypress groves?

Among the sinuous, flame-tall cypresses
That swayed their length of darkness all around
Etruscan-dusky, wavering men of old Etruria:
Naked except for fanciful long shoes,
Going with insidious, half-smiling quietness
And some of Africa's imperturbable sang-froid
About a forgotten business.

What business, then?
Nay, tongues are dead, and words are hollow as hollow
    seed-pods,
Having shed their sound and finished all their echoing
Etruscan syllables,
That had the telling.

Yet more I see you darkly concentrate,
Tuscan cypresses,
On one old thought:
On one old slim imperishable thought, while you remain
Etruscan cypresses;
Dusky, slim marrow-thought of slender, flickering men of
    Etruria,
Whom Rome called vicious.

Vicious, dark cypresses:
Vicious, you supple, brooding, softly-swaying pillars of
    dark flame.
Monumental to a dead, dead race
Embalmed in you!

Were they then vicious, the slender, tender-footed,
Long-nosed men of Etruria?
Or was their way only evasive and different, dark, like
    cypress-trees in a wind?

They are dead, with all their vices,
And all that is left
Is the shadowy monomania of some cypresses
And tombs.

The smile, the subtle Etruscan smile still lurking
Within the tombs,
Etruscan cypresses.
He laughs longest who laughs last;
Nay, Leonardo only bungled the pure Etruscan smile.

What would I not give
To bring back the rare and orchid-like
Evil-yclept Etruscan?

For as to the evil
We have only Roman word for it,
Which I, being a little weary of Roman virtue,
Don't hang much weight on.

For oh, I know, in the dust where we have buried
The silenced races and all their abominations,
We have buried so much of the delicate magic of life.

There in the deeps
That churn the frankincense and ooze the myrrh,
Cypress shadowy,
Such an aroma of lost human life!

They say the fit survive,
But I invoke the spirits of the lost.
Those that have not survived, the darkly lost,
To bring their meaning back into life again,
Which they have taken away
And wrapt inviolable in soft cypress-trees,
Etruscan cypresses.

Evil, what is evil?
There is only one evil, to deny life
As Rome denied Etruria
And mechanical America Montezuma still.

FIESOLE

FLOWERS

ALMOND BLOSSOM

Even iron can put forth,
Even iron.

This is the iron age,
But let us take heart
Seeing iron break and bud,
Seeing rusty iron puff with clouds of blossom.

The almond-tree,
December's bare iron hooks sticking out of earth.

The almond-tree,
That knows the deadliest poison, like a snake
In supreme bitterness.

Upon the iron, and upon the steel,
Odd flakes as if of snow, odd bits of snow,
Odd crumbs of melting snow.

But you mistake, it is not from the sky;
From out the iron, and from out the steel,
Flying not down from heaven, but storming up,
Strange storming up from the dense under-earth
Along the iron, to the living steel
In rose-hot tips, and flakes of rose-pale snow
Setting supreme annunciation to the world.

Nay, what a heart of delicate super-faith,
Iron-breaking,
The rusty swords of almond-trees.

Trees suffer, like races, down the long ages.
They wander and are exiled, they live in exile through long
        ages
Like drawn blades never sheathed, hacked and gone black
The alien trees in alien lands: and yet
The heart of blossom,
The unquenchable heart of blossom!

Look at the many-cicatrised frail vine, none more scarred
        and frail,

Yet see him fling himself abroad in fresh abandon
From the small wound-stump.

Even the wilful, obstinate, gummy fig-tree
Can be kept down, but he'll burst like a polyp into pro-
lixity.

And the almond-tree, in exile, in the iron age!

This is the ancient southern earth whence the vases were
    baked, amphoras, craters, cantharus, œnochœ, and
    open-hearted cylix,
Bristling now with the iron of almond-trees.

Iron, but unforgotten,
Iron, dawn-hearted,
Ever-beating dawn-heart, enveloped in iron against the
    exile, against the ages.

See it come forth in blossom
From the snow-remembering heart
In long-nighted January,
In the long dark nights of the evening star, and Sirius, and
    the Etna snow-wind through the long night.

Sweating his drops of blood through the long-nighted
    Gethsemane
Into blossom, into pride, into honey-triumph, into most
    exquisite splendour.
Oh, give me the tree of life in blossom
And the Cross sprouting its superb and fearless flowers!

Something must be reassuring to the almond, in the even-
    ing star, and the snow-wind, and the long, long,
    nights,
Some memory of far, sun-gentler lands,
So that the faith in his heart smiles again
And his blood ripples with that untellable delight of once-
    more-vindicated faith,

And the Gethsemane blood at the iron pores unfolds, un-
    folds,
Pearls itself into tenderness of bud
And in a great and sacred forthcoming steps forth, steps
    out in one stride
A naked tree of blossom, like a bridegroom bathing in dew,
    divested of cover,
Frail-naked, utterly uncovered
To the green night-baying of the dog-star, Etna's snow-
    edged wind
And January's loud-seeming sun.

Think of it, from the iron fastness
Suddenly to dare to come out naked, in perfection of
    blossom, beyond the sword-rust.
Think, to stand there in full-unfolded nudity, smiling,
With all the snow-wind, and the sun-glare, and the dog-star
    baying epithalamion.

Oh, honey-bodied beautiful one,
Come forth from iron,
Red your heart is.
Fragile-tender, fragile-tender life-body,
More fearless than iron all the time,
And so much prouder, so disdainful of reluctances.

In the distance like hoar-frost, like silvery ghosts com-
    muning on a green hill,
Hoar-frost-like and mysterious.

In the garden raying out
With a body like spray, dawn-tender, and looking about
With such insuperable, subtly-smiling assurance,
Sword-blade-born.

Unpromised,
No bounds being set.
Flaked out and come unpromised,

The tree being life-divine,
Fearing nothing, life-blissful at the core
Within iron and earth.

Knots of pink, fish-silvery
In heaven, in blue, blue heaven,
Soundless, bliss-full, wide-rayed, honey-bodied,
Red at the core,
Red at the core,
Knotted in heaven upon the fine light.

Open,
Open,
Five times wide open,
Six times wide open,
And given, and perfect;
And red at the core with the last sore-heartedness,
Sore-hearted-looking.

FONTANA VECCHIA

SICILIAN CYCLAMENS

WHEN he pushed his bush of black hair off his brow:
When she lifted her mop from her eyes, and screwed it in
    a knob behind
  – O act of fearful temerity!
When they felt their foreheads bare, naked to heaven, their
    eyes revealed:
When they felt the light of heaven brandished like a knife
    at their defenceless eyes,
And the sea like a blade at their face,
Mediterranean savages:
When they came out, face-revealed, under heaven, from the
    shaggy undergrowth of their own hair
For the first time,
They saw tiny rose cyclamens between their toes, growing
Where the slow toads sat brooding on the past.

Slow toads, and cyclamen leaves
Stickily glistening with eternal shadow
Keeping to earth.
Cyclamen leaves
Toad-filmy, earth-iridescent
Beautiful
Frost-filigreed
Spumed with mud
Snail-nacreous
Low down.

The shaking aspect of the sea
And man's defenceless bare face
And cyclamens putting their ears back.

Long, pensive, slim-muzzled greyhound buds
Dreamy, not yet present,
Drawn out of earth
At his toes.

Dawn-rose
Sub-delighted, stone-engendered
Cyclamens, young cyclamens
Arching
Waking, pricking their ears
Like delicate very-young greyhound bitches
Half-yawning at the open, inexperienced
Vista of day,
Folding back their soundless petalled ears.

Greyhound bitches
Bending their rosy muzzles pensive down,
And breathing soft, unwilling to wake to the new day
Yet sub-delighted.

Ah Mediterranean morning, when our world began!
Far-off Mediterranean mornings,

Pelasgic faces uncovered,
And unbudding cyclamens.

The hare suddenly goes uphill
Laying back her long ears with unwinking bliss.

And up the pallid, sea-blenched Mediterranean stone-slopes
Rose cyclamen, ecstatic fore-runner!
Cyclamens, ruddy-muzzled cyclamens
In little bunches like bunches of wild hares
Muzzles together, ears-aprick
Whispering witchcraft
Like women at a well, the dawn-fountain.

Greece, and the world's morning
Where all the Parthenon marbles still fostered the roots of
     the cyclamen.
Violets
Pagan, rosy-muzzled violets
Autumnal
Dawn-pink,
Dawn-pale
Among squat toad-leaves sprinkling the unborn
Erechtheion marbles.

TAORMINA

THE EVANGELISTIC BEASTS

ST MATTHEW

THEY are not all beasts.
One is a man, for example, and one is a bird.

I, Matthew, am a man.

'And I, if I be lifted up, will draw all men unto me' –

That is Jesus.
But then Jesus was not quite a man.

He was the Son of Man
Filius Meus, O remorseless logic
Out of His own mouth.

I, Matthew, being a man
Cannot be lifted up, the Paraclete
To draw all men unto me,
Seeing I am on a par with all men.

I, on the other hand,
Am drawn to the Uplifted, as all men are drawn,
To the Son of Man
Filius Meus.

Wilt thou lift me up, Son of Man?
How my heart beats!
I am man.

I am man, and therefore my heart beats, and throws the
      dark blood from side to side
All the time I am lifted up.

Yes, even during my uplifting.

And if it ceased?
If it ceased, I should be no longer man
As I am, if my heart in uplifting ceased to beat, to toss the
      dark blood from side to side, causing my myriad secret
      streams.

After the cessation
I might be a soul in bliss, an angel, approximating to the
      Uplifted;
But that is another matter;
I am Matthew, the man,
And I am not that other angelic matter.

So I will be lifted up, Saviour,
But put me down again in time, Master,
Before my heart stops beating, and I become what I am not.

Put me down again on the earth, Jesus, on the brown soil
Where flowers sprout in the acrid humus, and fade into
humus again.
Where beasts drop their unlicked young, and pasture, and
drop their droppings among the turf.
Where the adder darts horizontal.
Down on the damp, unceasing ground, where my feet
belong
And even my heart, Lord, forever, after all uplifting:
The crumbling, damp, fresh land, life horizontal and cease-
less.

Matthew I am, the man.
And I take the wings of the morning, to Thee, Crucified,
Glorified.
But while flowers club their petals at evening
And rabbits make pills among the short grass
And long snakes quickly glide into the dark hole in the
wall, hearing man approach,

I must be put down, Lord, in the afternoon,
And at evening I must leave off my wings of the spirit
As I leave off my braces,
And I must resume my nakedness like a fish, sinking down
the dark reversion of night
Like a fish seeking the bottom, Jesus,
ΙΧΘΥΣ
Face downwards
Veering slowly
Down between the steep slopes of darkness, fucus-dark,
seaweed-fringed valleys of the waters under the sea,
Over the edge of the soundless cataract
Into the fathomless, bottomless pit
Where my soul falls in the last throes of bottomless
convulsion, and is fallen
Utterly beyond Thee, Dove of the Spirit;
Beyond everything, except itself.

Nay, Son of Man, I have been lifted up.
To Thee I rose like a rocket ending in mid-heaven.
But even Thou, Son of Man, canst not quaff out the dregs of
     terrestrial manhood!
They fall back from Thee.

They fall back, and like a dripping of quicksilver taking the
     downward track,
Break into drops, burn into drops of blood, and dropping,
     dropping take wing
Membraned, blood-veined wings.
On fans of unsuspected tissue, like bats
They thread and thrill and flicker ever downward
To the dark zenith of Thine antipodes
Jesus Uplifted.

Bat-winged heart of man,
Reversed flame
Shuddering a strange way down the bottomless pit
To the great depths of its reversèd zenith.

Afterwards, afterwards
Morning comes, and I shake the dews of night from the
     wings of my spirit
And mount like a lark, Beloved.

But remember, Saviour,
That my heart which like a lark at heaven's gate singing,
     hovers morning-bright to Thee,
Throws still the dark blood back and forth
In the avenues where the bat hangs sleeping, upside-down
And to me undeniable, Jesus.

Listen, Paraclete.
I can no more deny the bat-wings of my fathom-flickering
     spirit of darkness
Than the wings of the Morning and Thee, Thou Glorified.

I am Matthew, the Man:
It is understood.
And Thou art Jesus, Son of Man
Drawing all men unto Thee, but bound to release them
    when the hour strikes.

I have been, and I have returned.
I have mounted up on the wings of the morning, and I have
    dredged down to the zenith's reversal.
Which is my way, being man.
Gods may stay in mid-heaven, the Son of Man has climbed
    to the Whitsun zenith,
But I, Matthew, being a man
Am a traveller back and forth.
So be it.

ST MARK

THERE was a lion in Judah
Which whelped, and was Mark.

But winged.
A lion with wings.
At least at Venice.
Even as late as Daniele Manin.

Why should he have wings?
Is he to be a bird also?
Or a spirit?
Or a winged thought?
Or a soaring consciousness?

Evidently he is all that
The lion of the spirit.

Ah, Lamb of God
Would a wingless lion lie down before Thee, as this winged
    lion lies?

The lion of the spirit.

Once he lay in the mouth of a cave
And sunned his whiskers,
And lashed his tail slowly, slowly
Thinking of voluptuousness
Even of blood.

But later, in the sun of the afternoon
Having tasted all there was to taste, and having slept his fill
He fell to frowning, as he lay with his head on his paws
And the sun coming in through the narrowest fibril of a
     slit in his eyes.

So, nine-tenths asleep, motionless, bored, and statically
     angry,
He saw in a shaft of light a lamb on a pinnacle, balancing a
   flag on its paw,
And he was thoroughly startled.

Going out to investigate
He found the lamb beyond him, on the inaccessible pin-
     nacle of light.
So he put his paw to his nose, and pondered.

'Guard my sheep,' came the silvery voice from the pinnacle,
'And I will give thee the wings of the morning.'
So the lion of blood thought it was worth it.

Hence he became a curly sheep-dog with dangerous pro-
     pensities
As Carpaccio will tell you:
Ramping round, guarding the flock of mankind,
Sharpening his teeth on the wolves,
Ramping up through the air like a kestrel
And lashing his tail above the world
And enjoying the sensation of heaven and righteousness
     and voluptuous wrath.

There is a new sweetness in his voluptuously licking his
    paw
Now that it is a weapon of heaven.
There is a new ecstasy in his roar of desirous love
Now that it sounds self-conscious through the unlimited
    sky.
He is well aware of himself
And he cherishes voluptuous delights, and thinks about
    them
And ceases to be a blood-thirsty king of beasts
And becomes the faithful sheep-dog of the Shepherd,
    thinking of his voluptuous pleasures of chasing the
    sheep to the fold
And increasing the flock, and perhaps giving a real nip
    here and there, a real pinch, but always well meant.

And somewhere there is a lioness
The she-mate.
Whelps play between the paws of the lion,
The she-mate purrs,
Their castle is impregnable, their cave,
The sun comes in their lair, they are well-off,
A well-to-do-family.

Then the proud lion stalks abroad, alone,
And roars to announce himself to the wolves
And also to encourage the red-cross Lamb
And chiefly to ensure a goodly increase in the world.

Look at him, with his paw on the world
At Venice and elsewhere.
Going blind at last.

ST LUKE

A WALL, a bastion,
A living forehead with its slow whorl of hair

And a bull's large, sombre, glancing eye
And glistening, adhesive muzzle
With cavernous nostrils where the winds run hot
Snorting defiance
Or greedily snuffling behind the cows.

Horns
The golden horns of power,
Power to kill, power to create
Such as Moses had, and God,
Head-power.

Shall great wings flame from his shoulder-sockets
Assyrian-wise?
It would be no wonder.

Knowing the thunder of his heart
The massive thunder of his dew-lapped chest
Deep and reverberating,
It would be no wonder if great wings, like flame, fanned
    out from the furnace-cracks of his shoulder-sockets.

Thud! Thud! Thud!
And the roar of black bull's blood in the mighty passages
    of his chest.

Ah, the dewlap swings pendulous with excess.
The great, roaring weight above
Like a furnace dripping a molten drip.

The urge, the massive, burning ache
Of the bull's breast.
The open furnace-doors of his nostrils.

For what does he ache, and groan?

In his breast a wall?

Nay, once it was also a fortress wall, and the weight of a
   vast battery.
But now it is a burning hearthstone only,
Massive old altar of his own burnt offering.

It was always an altar of burnt offering
His own black blood poured out like a sheet of flame over
   his fecundating herd
As he gave himself forth.

But also it was a fiery fortress frowning shaggily on the
   world
And announcing battle ready.

Since the Lamb bewitched him with that red-struck flag
His fortress is dismantled
His fires of wrath are banked down
His horns turn away from the enemy.

He serves the Son of Man.

And hear him bellow, after many years, the bull that serves
   the Son of Man.
Moaning, booing, roaring hollow
Constrained to pour forth all his fire down the narrow
   sluice of procreation
Through such narrow loins, too narrow.

Is he not over-charged by the dammed-up pressure of his
   own massive black blood
Luke, the Bull, the father of substance, the Providence Bull,
   after two thousand years?
Is he not overful of offering, a vast, vast offer of himself
Which must be poured through so small a vent?

Too small a vent.

Let him remember his horns, then.
Seal up his forehead once more to a bastion,

Let it know nothing.
Let him charge like a mighty catapult on the red-cross flag,
    let him roar out challenge on the world
And throwing himself upon it, throw off the madness of
    his blood.

Let it be war.

And so it is war.
The bull of the proletariat has got his head down.

ST JOHN

JOHN, oh John,
Thou honourable bird
Sun-peering eagle.

Taking a bird's-eye view
Even of Calvary and Resurrection
Not to speak of Babylon's whoredom.

High over the mild effulgence of the dove
Hung all the time, did we but know it, the all-knowing
    shadow
Of John's great gold-barred eagle.

John knew all about it
Even the very beginning.

'In the beginning was the Word
And the Word was God
And the Word was with God.'

Having been to school
John knew the whole proposition.
As for innocent Jesus
He was one of Nature's phenomena, no doubt.

Oh that mind-soaring eagle of an Evangelist
Staring creation out of countenance
And telling it off
As an eagle staring down on the Sun!

The Logos, the Logos!
'In the beginning was the Word.'

Is there not a great Mind pre-ordaining?
Does not a supreme Intellect ideally procreate the Universe?
Is not each soul a vivid thought in the great consciousness-
    stream of God?

Put salt on his tail
The sly bird of John.

Proud intellect, high-soaring Mind
Like a king eagle, bird of the most High, sweeping the
    round of heaven
And casting the cycles of creation
On two wings, like a pair of compasses;
Jesus' pale and lambent dove, cooing in the lower boughs
On sufferance.

In the beginning was the Word, of course.
And the word was the first offspring of the almighty
    Johannine mind,
Chick of the intellectual eagle.

Yet put salt on the tail of the Johannine bird,
Put salt on its tail
John's eagle.

Shoo it down out of the empyrean
Of the all-seeing, all-fore-ordaining ideal.
Make it roost on bird-spattered, rocky Patmos
And let it moult there, among the stones of the bitter sea.

For the almighty eagle of the fore-ordaining Mind
Is looking rather shabby and island-bound these days:
Moulting, and rather naked about the rump, and down in
    the beak,
Rather dirty, on dung-whitened Patmos.

From which we are led to assume
That the old bird is weary, and almost willing
That a new chick should chip the extensive shell
Of the mundane egg.

The poor old golden eagle of the creative spirit
Moulting and moping and waiting, willing at last
For the fire to burn it up, feathers and all
So that a new conception of the beginning and end
Can rise from the ashes.

Ah Phœnix, Phœnix
John's Eagle!
You are only known to us now as the badge of an insur-
    ance Company.

Phœnix, Phœnix
The nest is in flames
Feathers are singeing,
Ash flutters flocculent, like down on a blue, wan fledgeling.

SAN GERVASIO

CREATURES

MOSQUITO

WHEN did you start your tricks,
Monsieur?

What do you stand on such high legs for?
Why this length of shredded shank,
You exaltation?

Is it so that you shall lift your centre of gravity upwards
And weigh no more than air as you alight upon me,
Stand upon me weightless, you phantom?

I heard a woman call you the Winged Victory
In sluggish Venice.
You turn your head towards your tail, and smile.

How can you put so much devilry
Into that translucent phantom shred
Of a frail corpus?

Queer, with your thin wings and your streaming legs
How you sail like a heron, or a dull clot of air,
A nothingness.

Yet what an aura surrounds you;
Your evil little aura, prowling, and casting a numbness on
    my mind.

That is your trick, your bit of filthy magic:
Invisibility, and the anæsthetic power
To deaden my attention in your direction.

But I know your game now, streaky sorcerer.

Queer, how you stalk and prowl the air
In circles and evasions, enveloping me,
Ghoul on wings
Winged Victory.

Settle, and stand on long thin shanks
Eyeing me sideways, and cunningly conscious that I am
    aware,
You speck.

I hate the way you lurch off sideways into air
Having read my thoughts against you.

Come then, let us play at unawares,
And see who wins in this sly game of bluff,
Man or mosquito.

You don't know that I exist, and I don't know that you
    exist.
Now then!

It is your trump,
It is your hateful little trump,
You pointed fiend,
Which shakes my sudden blood to hatred of you:
It is your small, high, hateful bugle in my ear.

Why do you do it?
Surely it is bad policy.

They say you can't help it.

If that is so, then I believe a little in Providence protecting
    the innocent.
But it sounds so amazingly like a slogan,
A yell of triumph as you snatch my scalp.

Blood, red blood
Super-magical
Forbidden liquor.

I behold you stand
For a second enspasmed in oblivion,
Obscenely ecstasied
Sucking live blood,
My blood.

Such silence, such suspended transport,
Such gorging,
Such obscenity of trespass.

You stagger
As well as you may.

Only your accursed hairy frailty,
Your own imponderable weightlessness
Saves you, wafts you away on the very draught my anger
    makes in its snatching.

Away with a pæan of derision,
You winged blood-drop.

Can I not overtake you?
Are you one too many for me,
Winged Victory?
Am I not mosquito enough to out-mosquito you?

Queer, what a big stain my sucked blood makes
Beside the infinitesimal faint smear of you!
Queer, what a dim dark smudge you have disappeared into!

SIRACUSA

FISH

FISH, oh Fish,
So little matters!

Whether the waters rise and cover the earth
Or whether the waters wilt in the hollow places,
All one to you.

Aqueous, subaqueous,
Submerged
And wave-thrilled.

As the waters roll
Roll you.
The waters wash,
You wash in oneness
And never emerge.

Never know,
Never grasp.

Your life a sluice of sensation along your sides,
A flush at the flails of your fins, down the whorl of your
    tail,
And water wetly on fire in the grates of your gills;
Fixed water-eyes.

Even snakes lie together.

But oh, fish, that rock in water,
You lie only with the waters;
One touch.

No fingers, no hands and feet, no lips;
No tender muzzles,
No wistful bellies,
No loins of desire,
None.

You and the naked element,
Sway-wave.
Curvetting bits of tin in the evening light.

Who is it ejects his sperm to the naked flood?
In the wave-mother?
Who swims enwombed?
Who lies with the waters of his silent passion, womb-
    element?
– Fish in the waters under the earth.

What price *his* bread upon the waters?

Himself all silvery himself
In the element
No more.

Nothing more.

Himself,
And the element.

Food, of course!
Water-eager eyes,
Mouth-gate open
And strong spine urging, driving;
And desirous belly gulping.

Fear also!
He knows fear!
Water-eyes craning,
A rush that almost screams,
Almost fish-voice
As the pike comes . . .
Then gay fear, that turns the tail sprightly, from a shadow.

Food, and fear, and joie de vivre,
Without love.

The other way about:
Joie de vivre, and fear, and food,
All without love.

Quelle joie de vivre
Dans l'eau!
Slowly to gape through the waters,
Alone with the element;
To sink, and rise, and go to sleep with the waters;
To speak endless inaudible wavelets into the wave;
To breathe from the flood at the gills,
Fish-blood slowly running next to the flood, extracting
    fish-fire;
To have the element under one, like a lover;
And to spring away with a curvetting click in the air,
Provocative.
Dropping back with a slap on the face of the flood.
And merging oneself!

To be a fish!

So utterly without misgiving
To be a fish
In the waters.

Loveless, and so lively!
Born before God was love,
Or life knew loving.
Beautifully beforehand with it all.

Admitted, they swarm in companies,
Fishes.
They drive in shoals.
But soundless, and out of contact.
They exchange no word, no spasm, not even anger.
Not one touch.
Many suspended together, forever apart,
Each one alone with the waters, upon one wave with the
    rest.

A magnetism in the water between them only.

I saw a water-serpent swim across the Anapo,
And I said to my heart, *look, look at him!*
With his head up, steering like a bird!
He's a rare one, but he belongs . . .

But sitting in a boat on the Zeller lake
And watching the fishes in the breathing waters
Lift and swim and go their way –

I said to my heart, *who are these?*
And my heart couldn't own them . . .

A slim young pike, with smart fins
And grey-striped suit, a young cub of a pike
Slouching along away below, half out of sight,
Like a lout on an obscure pavement . . .

Aha, there's somebody in the know!

But watching closer
That motionless deadly motion,
That unnatural barrel body, that long ghoul nose, ..
I left off hailing him.

I had made a mistake, I didn't know him,
This grey, monotonous soul in the water,
This intense individual in shadow,
Fish-alive.

I didn't know his God,
I didn't know his God.

Which is perhaps the last admission that life has to wring
    out of us.

I saw, dimly,
Once a big pike rush,
And small fish fly like splinters.
And I said to my heart, *there are limits*
To you, my heart;
And to the one God.
Fish are beyond me.

Other Gods
Beyond my range ... gods beyond my God ...

They are beyond me, are fishes.
I stand at the pale of my being
And look beyond, and see
Fish, in the outerwards,
As one stands on a bank and looks in.

I have waited with a long rod
And suddenly pulled a gold-and-greenish, lucent fish from
    below,
And had him fly like a halo round my head,
Lunging in the air on the line.

Unhooked his gorping, water-horny mouth,
And seen his horror-tilted eye,
His red-gold, water-precious, mirror-flat bright eye;
And felt him beat in my hand, with his mucous, leaping
    life-throb.

And my heart accused itself
Thinking: *I am not the measure of creation.*
This is beyond me, this fish.
His God stands outside my God.

And the gold-and-green pure lacquer-mucous comes off in
    my hand,
And the red-gold mirror-eye stares and dies,
And the water-suave contour dims.

But not before I have had to know
He was born in front of my sunrise,
Before my day.

He outstarts me.
And I, a many-fingered horror of daylight to him,
Have made him die.

Fishes,
With their gold, red eyes, and green-pure gleam, and under-
    gold,
And their pre-world loneliness,
And more-than-lovelessness,
And white meat;
They move in other circles.

Outsiders.
Water-wayfarers.
Things of one element.
Aqueous,
Each by itself.

Cats, and the Neapolitans,
Sulphur sun-beasts,
Thirst for fish as for more-than-water;
Water-alive
To quench their over-sulphureous lusts.

But I, I only wonder
And don't know.
I don't know fishes.

In the beginning
Jesus was called The Fish. . . .
And in the end.

ZELL-AM-SEE

MAN AND BAT

WHEN I went into my room, at mid-morning,
Say ten o'clock . . .
My room, a crash-box over that great stone rattle
The Via de' Bardi . . .

When I went into my room at mid-morning
Why? . . . a bird!

A bird
Flying round the room in insane circles.

In insane circles!
. . . A bat!

A disgusting bat
At mid-morning! . . .

Out! Go out!

Round and round and round
With a twitchy, nervous, intolerable flight,
And a neurasthenic lunge,
And an impure frenzy;
A bat, big as a swallow!

Out, out of my room!

The venetian shutters I push wide
To the free, calm upper air;
Loop back the curtains . . .

Now out, out from my room!

So to drive him out, flicking with my white handkerchief:
    Go!
But he will not.

Round and round and round
In an impure haste,
Fumbling, a beast in air,
And stumbling, lunging and touching the walls, the bell-
    wires
About my room!

Always refusing to go out into the air
Above that crash-gulf of the Via de' Bardi,
Yet blind with frenzy, with cluttered fear.

At last he swerved into the window bay,
But blew back, as if an incoming wind blew him in again.
A strong inrushing wind.

And round and round and round!
Blundering more insane, and leaping, in throbs, to clutch
    at a corner,
At a wire, at a bell-rope:
On and on, watched relentless by me, round and round in
    my room,
Round and round and dithering with tiredness and haste
    and increasing delirium
Flicker-splashing round my room.

I would not let him rest;
Not one instant cleave, cling like a blot with his breast to
    the wall

In an obscure corner.
Not an instant!

I flicked him on,
Trying to drive him through the window.

Again he swerved into the window bay
And I ran forward, to frighten him forth.
But he rose, and from a terror worse than me he flew past
    me
Back into my room, and round, round, round in my room
Clutch, cleave, stagger,
Dropping about the air
Getting tired.

Something seemed to blow him back from the window
Every time he swerved at it;
Back on a strange parabola, then round, round, dizzy in my
    room.

He *could* not go out;
I also realised . . .

It was the light of day which he could not enter,
Any more than I could enter the white-hot door of a
    blast-furnace.
He could not plunge into the daylight that streamed at the
    window.
It was asking too much of his nature.

Worse even than the hideous terror of me with my hand-
    kerchief
Saying: *Out, go out!* . . .
Was the horror of white daylight in the window!

So I switched on the electric light, thinking: *Now*
The outside will seem brown . . .

But no.
The outside did not seem brown.
And he did not mind the yellow electric light.

Silent!
He was having a silent rest.
But never!
Not in my room.

Round and round and round
Near the ceiling as if in a web
Staggering;
Plunging, falling out of the web,
Broken in heaviness,
Lunging blindly,
Heavier;
And clutching, clutching for one second's pause,
Always, as if for one drop of rest,
One little drop.

And I!
Never, I say . . .
Go out!

Flying slower,
Seeming to stumble, to fall in air.
Blind-weary.

Yet never able to pass the whiteness of light into free-
dom . . .
A bird would have dashed through, come what might.

Fall, sink, lurch, and round and round
Flicker, flicker-heavy;
Even wings heavy:
And cleave in a high corner for a second, like a clot, also a
prayer.

But no.
Out, you beast.

Till he fell in a corner, palpitating, spent.
And there, a clot, he squatted and looked at me.
With sticking-out, bead-berry eyes, black,
And improper derisive ears,
And shut wings,
And brown, furry body.

Brown, nut-brown, fine fur!
But it might as well have been hair on a spider; thing
With long, black-paper ears.

So, a dilemma!
He squatted there like something unclean.

No, he must not squat, nor hang, obscene, in my room!

Yet nothing on earth will give him courage to pass the
     sweet fire of day.

What then?
Hit him and kill him and throw him away?

Nay,
I didn't create him.
Let the God that created him be responsible for his death ...
Only, in the bright day, I will not have this clot in my room.

Let the God who is maker of bats watch with them in their
     unclean corners ...
I admit a God in every crevice,
But not bats in my room;
Nor the God of bats, while the sun shines.

So out, out you brute! ...
And he lunged, flight-heavy, away from me, sideways,
     a sghembo!

And round and round and round my room, a clot with
    wings
Impure even in weariness.

Wings dark skinny and flapping the air,
Lost their flicker.
Spent.

He fell again with a little thud
Near the curtain on the floor.
And there lay.

Ah, death, death,
You are no solution!
Bats must be bats.

Only life has a way out.
And the human soul is fated to wide-eyed responsibility
In life.

So I picked him up in a flannel jacket,
Well covered, lest he should bite me.
For I would have had to kill him if he'd bitten me, the
    impure one . . .
And he hardly stirred in my hand, muffled up.

Hastily, I shook him out of the window.

And away he went!
Fear craven in his tail.
Great haste, and straight, almost bird straight above the
    Via de' Bardi.
Above that crash-gulf of exploding whips,
Towards the Borgo San Jacopo.

And now, at evening, as he flickers over the river
Dipping with petty triumphant flight, and tittering over
    the sun's departure,

I believe he chirps, pipistrello, seeing me here on this
terrace writing:
There he sits, the long loud one!
But I am greater than he ...
I escaped him ...

REPTILES

SNAKE

A SNAKE came to my water-trough
On a hot, hot day, and I in pyjamas for the heat,
To drink there.

In the deep, strange-scented shade of the great dark carob
tree
I came down the steps with my pitcher
And must wait, must stand and wait, for there he was at
the trough before me.

He reached down from a fissure in the earth-wall in the
gloom
And trailed his yellow-brown slackness soft-bellied down,
over the edge of the stone trough
And rested his throat upon the stone bottom,
And where the water had dripped from the tap, in a small
clearness,
He sipped with his straight mouth,
Softly drank through his straight gums, into his slack long
body,
Silently.

Someone was before me at my water-trough,
And I, like a second-comer, waiting.

He lifted his head from his drinking, as cattle do,
And looked at me vaguely, as drinking cattle do,

And flickered his two-forked tongue from his lips, and
    mused a moment,
And stooped and drank a little more,
Being earth-brown, earth-golden from the burning bowels
    of the earth
On the day of Sicilian July, with Etna smoking.

The voice of my education said to me
He must be killed,
For in Sicily the black, black snakes are innocent, the gold
    are venomous.

And voices in me said, If you were a man
You would take a stick and break him now, and finish him
    off.

But must I confess how I liked him,
How glad I was he had come like a guest in quiet, to drink
    at my water-trough
And depart peaceful, pacified, and thankless,
Into the burning bowels of this earth?

Was it cowardice, that I dared not kill him?
Was it perversity, that I longed to talk to him?
Was it humility, to feel so honoured?
I felt so honoured.

And yet those voices:
If you were not afraid, you would kill him!

And truly I was afraid, I was most afraid,
But even so, honoured still more
That he should seek my hospitality
From out the dark door of the secret earth.

He drank enough
And lifted his head, dreamily, as one who has drunken,

And flickered his tongue like a forked night on the air, so
    black,
Seeming to lick his lips,
And looked around like a god, unseeing, into the air,
And slowly turned his head,
And slowly, very slowly, as if thrice adream,
Proceeded to draw his slow length curving round
And climb again the broken bank of my wall-face.

And as he put his head into that dreadful hole,
And as he slowly drew up, snake-easing his shoulders, and
    entered farther,
A sort of horror, a sort of protest against his withdrawing
    into that horrid black hole,
Deliberately going into the blackness, and slowly drawing
    himself after,
Overcame me now his back was turned.

I looked round, I put down my pitcher,
I picked up a clumsy log
And threw it at the water-trough with a clatter.

I think it did not hit him,
But suddenly that part of him that was left behind con-
    vulsed in undignified haste,
Writhed like lightning, and was gone
Into the black hole, the earth-lipped fissure in the wall-
    front,
At which, in the intense still noon, I stared with fascination.

And immediately I regretted it.
I thought how paltry, how vulgar, what a mean act!
I despised myself and the voices of my accursed human
    education.

And I thought of the albatross,
And I wished he would come back, my snake.

For he seemed to me again like a king,
Like a king in exile, uncrowned in the underworld,
Now due to be crowned again.

And so, I missed my chance with one of the lords
Of life.
And I have something to expiate:
A pettiness.

TAORMINA

TORTOISES

BABY TORTOISE

You know what it is to be born alone,
Baby tortoise!

The first day to heave your feet little by little from the shell,
Not yet awake,
And remain lapsed on earth,
Not quite alive.

A tiny, fragile, half-animate bean.

To open your tiny beak-mouth, that looks as if it would
    never open,
Like some iron door;
To lift the upper hawk-beak from the lower base
And reach your skinny little neck
And take your first bite at some dim bit of herbage,
Alone, small insect,
Tiny bright-eye,
Slow one.

To take your first solitary bite
And move on your slow, solitary hunt.
Your bright, dark little eye,
Your eye of a dark disturbed night,

Under its slow lid, tiny baby tortoise,
So indomitable.

No one ever heard you complain.

You draw your head forward, slowly, from your little
    wimple
And set forward, slow-dragging, on your four-pinned toes,
Rowing slowly forward.
Whither away, small bird?

Rather like a baby working its limbs,
Except that you make slow, ageless progress
And a baby makes none.

The touch of sun excites you,
And the long ages, and the lingering chill
Make you pause to yawn,
Opening your impervious mouth,
Suddenly beak-shaped, and very wide, like some suddenly
    gaping pincers;
Soft red tongue, and hard thin gums,
Then close the wedge of your little mountain front,
Your face, baby tortoise.

Do you wonder at the world, as slowly you turn your head
    in its wimple
And look with laconic, black eyes?
Or is sleep coming over you again,
The non-life?

You are so hard to wake.

Are you able to wonder?
Or is it just your indomitable will and pride of the first life
Looking round
And slowly pitching itself against the inertia
Which had seemed invincible?

The vast inanimate,
And the fine brilliance of your so tiny eye,
Challenger.

Nay, tiny shell-bird,
What a huge vast inanimate it is, that you must row against,
What an incalculable inertia.

Challenger,
Little Ulysses, fore-runner,
No bigger than my thumb-nail,
Buon viaggio.

All animate creation on your shoulder,
Set forth, little Titan, under your battle-shield.

The ponderous, preponderate,
Inanimate universe;
And you are slowly moving, pioneer, you alone.

How vivid your travelling seems now, in the troubled
  sunshine,
Stoic, Ulyssean atom;
Suddenly hasty, reckless, on high toes.

Voiceless little bird,
Resting your head half out of your wimple
In the slow dignity of your eternal pause.
Alone, with no sense of being alone,
And hence six times more solitary;
Fulfilled of the slow passion of pitching through
  immemorial ages
Your little round house in the midst of chaos.

Over the garden earth,
Small bird,
Over the edge of all things.

Traveller,
With your tail tucked a little on one side
Like a gentleman in a long-skirted coat.

All life carried on your shoulder,
Invincible fore-runner.

TORTOISE-SHELL

THE Cross, the Cross
Goes deeper in than we know,
Deeper into life;
Right into the marrow
And through the bone.

Along the back of the baby tortoise
The scales are locked in an arch like a bridge,
Scale-lapping, like a lobster's sections
Or a bee's.

Then crossways down his sides
Tiger-stripes and wasp-bands.

Five, and five again, and five again,
And round the edges twenty-five little ones,
The sections of the baby tortoise shell.

Four, and a keystone;
Four, and a keystone;
Four, and a keystone;
Then twenty-four, and a tiny little keystone.

It needed Pythagoras to see life playing with counters on
the living back
Of the baby tortoise;
Life establishing the first eternal mathematical tablet,
Not in stone, like the Judean Lord, or bronze, but in life-
clouded, life-rosy tortoise shell.

The first little mathematical gentleman
Stepping, wee mite, in his loose trousers
Under all the eternal dome of mathematical law.

Fives, and tens,
Threes and fours and twelves,
All the *volte face* of decimals,
The whirligig of dozens and the pinnacle of seven.

Turn him on his back,
The kicking little beetle,
And there again, on his shell-tender, earth-touching belly,
The long cleavage of division, upright of the eternal cross
And on either side count five,
On each side, two above, on each side, two below
The dark bar horizontal.

The Cross!
It goes right through him, the sprottling insect,
Through his cross-wise cloven psyche,
Through his five-fold complex-nature.

So turn him over on his toes again;
Four pin-point toes, and a problematical thumb-piece,
Four rowing limbs, and one wedge-balancing head,
Four and one makes five, which is the clue to all mathe-
    matics.

The Lord wrote it all down on the little slate
Of the baby tortoise.
Outward and visible indication of the plan within,
The complex, manifold involvedness of an individual
    creature
Plotted out
On this small bird, this rudiment,
This little dome, this pediment
Of all creation,
This slow one.

On he goes, the little one,
Bud of the universe,
Pediment of life.

Setting off somewhere, apparently.
Whither away, brisk egg?

His mother deposited him on the soil as if he were no more
    than droppings,
And now he scuffles tinily past her as if she were an old
    rusty tin.

A mere obstacle,
He veers round the slow great mound of her –
Tortoises always foresee obstacles.

It is no use my saying to him in an emotional voice:
'This is your Mother, she laid you when you were an egg.'

He does not even trouble to answer: 'Woman, what have I
    to do with thee?'
He wearily looks the other way,
And she even more wearily looks another way still,
Each with the utmost apathy,
Incognizant,
Unaware,
Nothing.

As for papa,
He snaps when I offer him his offspring,
Just as he snaps when I poke a bit of stick at him,
Because he is irascible this morning, an irascible tortoise
Being touched with love, and devoid of fatherliness.

Father and mother,
And three little brothers,

And all rambling aimless, like little perambulating pebbles
    scattered in the garden,
Not knowing each other from bits of earth or old tins.

Except that papa and mama are old acquaintances, of course,
Though family feeling there is none, not even the begin-
    nings.

Fatherless, motherless, brotherless, sisterless
Little tortoise.

Row on then, small pebble,
Over the clods of the autumn, wind-chilled sunshine,
Young gaiety.

Does he look for a companion?

No, no, don't think it.
He doesn't know he is alone;
Isolation is his birthright,
This atom.

To row forward, and reach himself tall on spiny toes,
To travel, to burrow into a little loose earth, afraid of the
    night,
To crop a little substance,
To move, and to be quite sure that he is moving:
Basta!
To be a tortoise!
Think of it, in a garden of inert clods
A brisk, brindled little tortoise, all to himself –
Crœsus!

In a garden of pebbles and insects
To roam, and feel the slow heart beat
Tortoise-wise, the first bell sounding
From the warm blood, in the dark-creation morning.

Moving, and being himself,
Slow, and unquestioned,
And inordinately there, O stoic!
Wandering in the slow triumph of his own existence,
Ringing the soundless bell of his presence in chaos,
And biting the frail grass arrogantly,
Decidedly arrogantly.

LUI ET ELLE

SHE is large and matronly
And rather dirty,
A little sardonic-looking, as if domesticity had driven her
    to it.

Though what she does, except lay four eggs at random in
    the garden once a year
And put up with her husband,
I don't know.

She likes to eat.
She hurries up, striding reared on long uncanny legs,
When food is going.
Oh yes, she can make haste when she likes.

She snaps the soft bread from my hand in great mouthfuls,
Opening her rather pretty wedge of an iron, pristine face
Into an enormously wide-beaked mouth
Like sudden curved scissors,
And gulping at more than she can swallow, and working
    her thick, soft tongue,
And having the bread hanging over her chin.

O Mistress, Mistress,
Reptile mistress,
Your eye is very dark, very bright,
And it never softens
Although you watch.

She knows,
She knows well enough to come for food,
Yet she sees me not;
Her bright eye sees, but not me, not anything,
Sightful, sightless, seeing and visionless,
Reptile mistress.

Taking bread in her curved, gaping, toothless mouth,
She has no qualm when she catches my finger in her steel
overlapping gums,
But she hangs on, and my shout and my shrinking are
nothing to her,
She does not even know she is nipping me with her curved
beak.
Snake-like she draws at my finger, while I drag it in horror
away.

Mistress, reptile mistress,
You are almost too large, I am almost frightened.

He is much smaller,
Dapper beside her,
And ridiculously small.

Her laconic eye has an earthy, materialistic look,
His, poor darling, is almost fiery.

His wimple, his blunt-prowed face,
His low forehead, his skinny neck, his long, scaled, striving
legs,
So striving, striving,
Are all more delicate than she,
And he has a cruel scar on his shell.

Poor darling, biting at her feet,
Running beside her like a dog, biting her earthy, splay
feet,

Nipping her ankles,
Which she drags apathetic away, though without retreating
    into her shell.

Agelessly silent,
And with a grim, reptile determination,
Cold, voiceless age-after-age behind him, serpents' long
    obstinacy
Of horizontal persistence.

Little old man
Scuffling beside her, bending down, catching his oppor-
    tunity,
Parting his steel-trap face, so suddenly, and seizing her
    scaly ankle,
And hanging grimly on,
Letting go at last as she drags away,
And closing his steel-trap face.

His steel-trap, stoic, ageless, handsome face.
Alas, what a fool he looks in this scuffle.

And how he feels it!
The lonely rambler, the stoic, dignified stalker through
    chaos,
The immune, the animate,
Enveloped in isolation,
Forerunner.
Now look at him!

Alas, the spear is through the side of his isolation.
His adolescence saw him crucified into sex,
Doomed, in the long crucifixion of desire, to seek his
    consummation beyond himself.
Divided into passionate duality,
He, so finished and immune, now broken into desirous
    fragmentariness,

Doomed to make an intolerable fool of himself
In his effort toward completion again.

Poor little earthy house-inhabiting Osiris,
The mysterious bull tore him at adolescence into pieces,
And he must struggle after reconstruction, ignominiously.

And so behold him following the tail
Of that mud-hovel of his slowly rambling spouse,
Like some unhappy bull at the tail of a cow,
But with more than bovine, grim, earth-dank persistence,
Suddenly seizing the ugly ankle as she stretches out to
    walk,
Roaming over the sods,
Or, if it happen to show, at her pointed, heavy tail
Beneath the low-dropping back-board of her shell.

Their two shells like domed boats bumping,
Hers huge, his small;
Their splay feet rambling and rowing like paddles,
And stumbling mixed up in one another,
In the race of love –
Two tortoises,
She huge, he small.

She seems earthily apathetic,
And he has a reptile's awful persistence.

I heard a woman pitying her, pitying the Mère Tortue.
While I, I pity Monsieur.
'He pesters her and torments her,' said the woman.
How much more is *he* pestered and tormented, say I.

What can he do?
He is dumb, he is visionless,
Conceptionless.
His black, sad-lidded eye sees but beholds not
As her earthen mound moves on,

But he catches the folds of vulnerable, leathery skin,
Nail-studded, that shake beneath her shell,
And drags at these with his beak,
Drags and drags and bites,
While she pulls herself free, and rows her dull mound
    along.

TORTOISE GALLANTRY

MAKING his advances
He does not look at her, nor sniff at her,
No, not even sniff at her, his nose is blank.

Only he senses the vulnerable folds of skin
That work beneath her while she sprawls along
In her ungainly pace,
Her folds of skin that work and row
Beneath the earth-soiled hovel in which she moves.

And so he strains beneath her housey walls
And catches her trouser-legs in his beak
Suddenly, or her skinny limb,
And strange and grimly drags at her
Like a dog,
Only agelessly silent, with a reptile's awful persistency.

Grim, gruesome gallantry, to which he is doomed.
Dragged out of an eternity of silent isolation
And doomed to partiality, partial being,
Ache, and want of being,
Want,
Self-exposure, hard humiliation, need to add himself on to
    her.

Born to walk alone,
Fore-runner,

Now suddenly distracted into this mazy side-track,
This awkward, harrowing pursuit,
This grim necessity from within.

Does she know
As she moves eternally slowly away?
Or is he driven against her with a bang, like a bird flying in
    the dark against a window,
All knowledgeless?

The awful concussion,
And the still more awful need to persist, to follow, follow,
    continue,
Driven, after æons of pristine, fore-god-like singleness and
    oneness,
At the end of some mysterious, red-hot iron,
Driven away from himself into her tracks,
Forced to crash against her.

Stiff, gallant, irascible, crook-legged reptile,
Little gentleman,
Sorry plight,
We ought to look the other way.

Save that, having come with you so far,
We will go on to the end.

TORTOISE SHOUT

I THOUGHT he was dumb,
I said he was dumb,
Yet I've heard him cry.

First faint scream,
Out of life's unfathomable dawn,
Far off, so far, like a madness, under the horizon's dawning
    rim,
Far, far off, far scream.

Tortoise *in extremis*.

Why were we crucified into sex?
Why were we not left rounded off, and finished in our-
selves,
As we began,
As he certainly began, so perfectly alone?

A far, was-it-audible scream,
Or did it sound on the plasm direct?

Worse than the cry of the new-born,
A scream,
A yell,
A shout,
A pæan,
A death-agony,
A birth-cry,
A submission,
All tiny, tiny, far away, reptile under the first dawn.

War-cry, triumph, acute-delight, death-scream reptilian,
Why was the veil torn?
The silken shriek of the soul's torn membrane?
The male soul's membrane
Torn with a shriek half music, half horror.

Crucifixion.
Male tortoise, cleaving behind the hovel-wall of that dense
female,
Mounted and tense, spread-eagle, out-reaching out of the
shell
In tortoise-nakedness,
Long neck, and long vulnerable limbs extruded, spread-
eagle over her house-roof,
And the deep, secret, all-penetrating tail curved beneath
her walls,

Reaching and gripping tense, more reaching anguish in
    uttermost tension
Till suddenly, in the spasm of coition, tupping like a jerking
    leap, and oh!
Opening its clenched face from his outstretched neck
And giving that fragile yell, that scream,
Super-audible,
From his pink, cleft, old-man's mouth,
Giving up the ghost,
Or screaming in Pentecost, receiving the ghost.

His scream, and his moment's subsidence,
The moment of eternal silence,
Yet unreleased, and after the moment, the sudden, startling
    jerk of coition, and at once
The inexpressible faint yell –
And so on, till the last plasm of my body was melted back
To the primeval rudiments of life, and the secret.

So he tups, and screams
Time after time that frail, torn scream
After each jerk, the longish interval,
The tortoise eternity,
Agelong, reptilian persistence,
Heart-throb, slow heart-throb, persistent for the next
    spasm.

I remember, when I was a boy,
I heard the scream of a frog, which was caught with his
    foot in the mouth of an up-starting snake;
I remember when I first heard bull-frogs break into sound
    in the spring;
I remember hearing a wild goose out of the throat of night
Cry loudly, beyond the lake of waters;
I remember the first time, out of a bush in the darkness, a
    nightingale's piercing cries and gurgles startled the
    depths of my soul;

I remember the scream of a rabbit as I went through a wood
    at midnight;
I remember the heifer in her heat, blorting and blorting
    through the hours, persistent and irrepressible;
I remember my first terror hearing the howl of weird,
    amorous cats;
I remember the scream of a terrified, injured horse, the
    sheet-lightning,
And running away from the sound of a woman in labour,
    something like an owl whooing,
And listening inwardly to the first bleat of a lamb,
The first wail of an infant,
And my mother singing to herself,
And the first tenor singing of the passionate throat of a
    young collier, who has long since drunk himself to
    death,
The first elements of foreign speech
On wild dark lips.

And more than all these,
And less than all these,
This last,
Strange, faint coition yell
Of the male tortoise at extremity,
Tiny from under the very edge of the farthest far-off
    horizon of life.

The cross,
The wheel on which our silence first is broken,
Sex, which breaks up our integrity, our single inviolability,
    our deep silence
Tearing a cry from us.

Sex, which breaks us into voice, sets us calling across the
    deeps, calling, calling for the complement,
Singing, and calling, and singing again, being answered,
    having found.

Torn, to become whole again, after long seeking for what is
lost,
The same cry from the tortoise as from Christ, the Osiris-cry
of abandonment,
That which is whole, torn asunder,
That which is in part, finding its whole again throughout
the universe.

BIRDS

TURKEY-COCK

You ruffled black blossom,
You glossy dark wind.

Your sort of gorgeousness,
Dark and lustrous
And skinny repulsive
And poppy-glossy,
Is the gorgeousness that evokes my most puzzled admira-
tion.

Your aboriginality
Deep, unexplained,
Like a Red Indian darkly unfinished and aloof,
Seems like the black and glossy seeds of countless cen-
turies.

Your wattles are the colour of steel-slag which has been
red-hot
And is going cold,
Cooling to a powdery, pale-oxidised sky-blue.

Why do you have wattles, and a naked, wattled head?
Why do you arch your naked-set eye with a more-than-
comprehensible arrogance?

The vulture is bald, so is the condor, obscenely,
But only you have thrown this amazing mantilla of oxi-
    dised sky-blue
And hot red over you.

This queer dross shawl of blue and vermilion,
Whereas the peacock has a diadem.

I wonder why.
Perhaps it is a sort of uncanny decoration, a veil of loose
    skin.
Perhaps it is your assertion, in all this ostentation, of raw
    contradictoriness.
Your wattles drip down like a shawl to your breast
And the point of your mantilla drops across your nose,
    unpleasantly.

Or perhaps it is something unfinished
A bit of slag still adhering, after your firing in the furnace
    of creation.

Or perhaps there is something in your wattles of a bull's
    dew-lap
Which slips down like a pendulum to balance the throbbing
    mass of a generous breast,
The over-drip of a great passion hanging in the balance.
Only yours would be a raw, unsmelted passion, that will not
    quite fuse from the dross.

You contract yourself,
You arch yourself as an archer's bow
Which quivers indrawn as you clench your spine
Until your veiled head almost touches backward
To the root-rising of your erected tail.
And one intense and backward-curving frisson
Seizes you as you clench yourself together
Like some fierce magnet bringing its poles together.

Burning, pale positive pole of your wattled head!
And from the darkness of that opposite one
The upstart of your round-barred, sun-round tail!

Whilst between the two, along the tense arch of your back
Blows the magnetic current in fierce blasts,
Ruffling black, shining feathers like lifted mail,
Shuddering storm wind, or a water rushing through.

Your brittle, super-sensual arrogance
Tosses the crape of red across your brow and down your
    breast
As you draw yourself upon yourself in insistence.

It is a declaration of such tension in will
As time has not dared to avouch, nor eternity been able to
    unbend
Do what it may.
A raw American will, that has never been tempered by life;
You brittle, will-tense bird with a foolish eye.

The peacock lifts his rods of bronze
And struts blue-brilliant out of the far East.
But watch a turkey prancing low on earth
Drumming his vaulted wings, as savages drum
Their rhythms on long-drawn, hollow, sinister drums.
The ponderous, sombre sound of the great drum of
    Huichilobos
In pyramid Mexico, during sacrifice.
Drum, and the turkey onrush,
Sudden, demonic dauntlessness, full abreast,
All the bronze gloss of all his myriad petals
Each one apart and instant.
Delicate frail crescent of the gentle outline of white
At each feather-tip
So delicate;
Yet the bronze wind-bell suddenly clashing
And the eye over-weening into madness.

Turkey-cock, turkey-cock
Are you the bird of the next dawn?

Has the peacock had his day, does he call in vain, screecher,
　　for the sun to rise?
The eagle, the dove, and the barnyard rooster, do they call
　　in vain, trying to wake the morrow?
And do you await us, wattled father, Westward?
Will your yell do it?

Take up the trail of the vanished American
Where it disappeared at the foot of the crucifix?
Take up the primordial Indian obstinacy,
The more than human, dense insistence of will,
And disdain, and blankness, and onrush, and prise open
　　the new day with them?

The East a dead letter, and Europe moribund ... Is that so?
And those sombre, dead, feather-lustrous Aztecs, Amer-
　　indians,
In all the sinister splendour of their red blood-sacrifices,
Do they stand under the dawn, half-godly, half-demon,
　　awaiting the cry of the turkey-cock?

Or must you go through the fire once more, till you're
　　smelted pure,
Slag-wattled turkey-cock,
Dross-jabot?

FIESOLE

HUMMING-BIRD

I CAN imagine, in some otherworld
Primeval-dumb, far back
In that most awful stillness, that only gasped and hummed,
Humming-birds raced down the avenues.

Before anything had a soul,
While life was a heave of Matter, half inanimate,
This little bit chipped off in brilliance
And went whizzing through the slow, vast, succulent
    stems.

I believe there were no flowers, then,
In the world where the humming-bird flashed ahead of
    creation.
I believe he pierced the slow vegetable veins with his long
    beak.

Probably he was big
As mosses, and little lizards, they say were once big.
Probably he was a jabbing, terrifying monster.

We look at him through the wrong end of the long tele-
    scope of Time,
Luckily for us.

                                        ESPAÑOLA

THE BLUE JAY

The blue jay with a crest on his head
Comes round the cabin in the snow.
He runs in the snow like a bit of blue metal,
Turning his back on everything.

From the pine-tree that towers and hisses like a pillar of
    shaggy cloud
Immense above the cabin
Comes a strident laugh as we approach, this little black dog
    and I,
So halts the little black bitch on four spread paws in the
    snow
And looks up inquiringly into the pillar of cloud,
With a tinge of misgiving.
Ca-a-a! comes the scrape of ridicule out of the tree.

What voice of the Lord is that, from the tree of smoke?

Oh Bibbles, little black bitch in the snow,
With a pinch of snow in the groove of your silly snub nose,
What do you look at *me* for?
What do you look at me for, with such misgiving?

It's the blue jay laughing at us.
It's the blue jay jeering at us, Bibs.

Every day since the snow is here
The blue jay paces round the cabin, very busy, picking up
     bits,
Turning his back on us all,
And bobbing his thick dark crest about the snow, as if
     darkly saying:
I ignore those folk who look out.

You acid-blue metallic bird,
You thick bird with a strong crest
Who are you?
Whose boss are you, with all your bully way?
You copper-sulphate blue-bird!

LOBO

ANIMALS

THE ASS

THE long-drawn bray of the ass
In the Sicilian twilight —

All mares are dead!
All mares are dead!
Oh-h!
Oh-h-h!
Oh-h-h-h-h — h!!
I can't bear it, I can't bear it,

I can't!
Oh, I can't!
Oh –
There's one left!
There's one left!
One!
There's one ... left ...

So ending on a grunt of agonised relief.

This is the authentic Arabic interpretation of the braying
    of the ass.
And Arabs should know.

And yet, as his brass-resonant howling yell resounds
    through the Sicilian twilight
I am not sure –

His big, furry head,
His big, regretful eyes,
His diminished, drooping hindquarters,
His small toes.

Such a dear!
Such an ass!
With such a knot inside him!
He regrets something that he remembers.
That's obvious.

The Steppes of Tartary,
And the wind in his teeth for a bit,
And *noli me tangere*.

Ah then, when he tore the wind with his teeth,
And trod wolves underfoot,
And over-rode his mares as if he were savagely leaping an
    obstacle, to set his teeth in the sun ...

Somehow, alas, he fell in love,
And was sold into slavery.

He fell into the rut of love,
Poor ass, like man, always in rut,
The pair of them alike in that.

All his soul in his gallant member
And his head gone heavy with the knowledge of desire
And humiliation.

The ass was the first of all animals to fall finally into love,
From obstacle-leaping pride,
Mare obstacle,
Into love, mare-goal, and the knowledge of love.

Hence Jesus rode him in the Triumphant Entry.
Hence his beautiful eyes.
Hence his ponderous head, brooding over desire, and
    downfall, Jesus, and a pack-saddle;
Hence he uncovers his big ass-teeth and howls in that
    agony that is half insatiable desire and half unquench-
    able humiliation.
Hence the black cross on his shoulders.

The Arabs were only half right, though they hinted the
    whole:
Everlasting lament in everlasting desire.

See him standing with his head down, near the Porta
    Cappucini.
Asinello,
Somaro;
With the half-veiled, beautiful eyes, and the pensive face
    not asleep,
Motionless, like a bit of rock.

Has he seen the Gorgon's head, and turned to stone?
Alas, Love did it.

Now he's a jackass, a pack-ass, a donkey, somaro, burro,
     with a boss piling loads on his back.
Tied by the nose at the Porta Cappucini.
And tied in a knot inside, deadlocked between two desires:
To overleap like a male all mares as obstacles
In a leap at the sun;
And to leap in one last heart-bursting leap like a male at
     the goal of a mare,
And there end.
Well, you can't have it both roads.

Hee! Hee! Ehee! Ehow! Ehaw!! Oh! Oh! Oh-h-h!!
The wave of agony bursts in the stone that he was,
Bares his long ass's teeth, flattens his long ass's ears,
     straightens his donkey neck,
And howls his pandemonium on the indignant air.

Yes, it's a quandary.
Jesus rode on him, the first burden on the first beast of
     burden.
Love on a submissive ass.
So the tale began.

But the ass never forgets.

The horse, being nothing but a nag, will forget.
And men, being mostly geldings and knacker-boned hacks,
     have almost all forgot.
But the ass is a primal creature, and never forgets.

The Steppes of Tartary,
And Jesus on a meek ass-colt: mares: Mary escaping to
     Egypt: Joseph's cudgel.

Hee! Hee! Ehee! Ehow-ow!-ow!-aw!-aw!-aw!
All mares are dead!
Or else I am dead!
One of us, or the pair of us,

163

I don't know-ow!-ow!
Which!
Not sure-ure-ure
Quite which!
Which!

TAORMINA

HE-GOAT

S<small>EE</small> his black nose snubbed back, pressed over like a
   whale's blow-holes,
As if his nostrils were going to curve back to the root of
   his tail.

As he charges slow among the herd
And rows among the females like a ship pertinaciously,
Heavy with a rancid cargo, through the lesser ships –
Old father
Sniffing forever ahead of him, at the rear of the goats, that
   they lift the little door;
And rowing on, unarrived, no matter how often he enter:
Like a big ship pushing her bow-sprit over the little ships
Then swerving and steering afresh
And never, never arriving at journey's end, at the rear of
   the female ships.

Yellow eyes incomprehensible with thin slits
To round-eyed us.

Yet if you had whorled horns of bronze in a frontal dark
   wall
At the end of a back-bone ridge, like a straight sierra
   roqueña,
And nerves urging forward to the wall, you'd have eyes
   like his,
Especially if, being given a needle's eye of egress elsewhere
You tried to look back to it, and couldn't.

164

Sometimes he turns with a start, to fight, to challenge, to
    suddenly butt.
And then you see the God that he is, in a cloud of black
    hair
And storm-lightning-slitted eye.
Splendidly planting his feet, one rocky foot striking the
    ground with a sudden rock-hammer announcement:

I am here!
And suddenly lowering his head, the whorls of bone and of
    horn
Slowly revolving towards unexploded explosion,
As from the stem of his bristling, lightning-conductor tail
In a rush up the shrieking duct of his vertebral way
Runs a rage drawn in from the ether divinely through him
Towards a shock and a crash and a smiting of horns ahead.

That is a grand old lust of his, to gather the great
Rage of the sullen-stagnating atmosphere of goats
And bring it hurtling to a head, with crash of horns against
    the horns
Of the opposite enemy goat,
Thus hammering the mettle of goats into proof, and
    smiting out
The godhead of goats from the shock.
Things of iron are beaten on the anvil,
And he-goat is anvil to he-goat, and hammer to he-goat
In the business of beating the mettle of goats to a god-head.

But they've taken his enemy from him
And left him only his libidinousness,
His nostrils turning back, to sniff at even himself
And his slitted eyes seeking the needle's eye,
His own, unthreaded, forever.

So it is, when they take the enemy from us,
And we can't fight.

He is not fatherly, like the bull, massive Providence of hot
blood;
The goat is an egoist, aware of himself, devilish aware of
himself,
And full of malice prepense, and overweening, determined
to stand on the highest peak
Like the devil, and look on the world as his own.

And as for love:
With a needle of long red flint he stabs in the dark
At the living rock he is up against;
While she with her goaty mouth stands smiling the while
as he strikes, since sure
He will never *quite* strike home, on the target-quick, for
her quick
Is just beyond the range of the arrow he shoots
From his leap at the zenith in her, so it falls just short of
the mark, far enough.
It is over before it is finished.
She, smiling with goaty munch-mouth, Mona Lisa,
arranges it so.

Orgasm after orgasm after orgasm
And he smells so rank, and his nose goes back,
And never an enemy brow-metalled to thresh it out with
in the open field;
Never a mountain peak, to be king of the castle.
Only those eternal females to overleap and surpass, and
never succeed.

The involved voluptousness of the soft-footed cat
Who is like a fur folding a fur,
The cat who laps blood, and knows
The soft welling of blood invincible even beyond bone or
metal of bone.
The soft, the secret, the unfathomable blood

The cat has lapped
And known it subtler than frisson-shaken nerves,
Stronger than multiplicity of bone on bone
And darker than even the arrows of violentest will
Can pierce, for that is where will gives out, like a sinking
    stone that can sink no further.

But he-goat,
Black procreant male of the selfish will and libidinous desire,
God in black cloud with curving horns of bronze,
Find an enemy, Egoist, and clash the cymbals in face-to-
    face defiance,
And let the lightning out of your smothered dusk.

Forget the female herd for a bit,
And fight to be boss of the world.
Fight, old Satan with a selfish will, fight for your selfish
    will;
Fight to be the devil on the tip of the peak
Overlooking the world for his own.

But bah, how can he, poor domesticated beast!

TAORMINA

SHE-GOAT

GOATS go past the back of the house like dry leaves in
    the dawn,
And up the hill like a river, if you watch.

At dusk they patter back like a bough being dragged on
    the ground,
Raising dust and acridity of goats, and bleating.

Our old goat we tie up at night in the shed at the back of
    the broken Greek tomb in the garden,
And when the herd goes by at dawn she begins to bleat for
    me to come down and untie her.

Merr-err-err! Merr-er-errr! Mer! Mé!
Wait, wait a bit, I'll come when I've lit the fire.
Merrr!
Exactly.
Mé! Mer! Merrrrrrr!!!
Tace, tu, crapa, bestia!
Merr-ererrr-ererrrr! Merrrr!

She is such an alert listener, with her ears wide, to know am
I coming!
Such a canny listener, from a distance, looking upwards,
lending first one ear, then another.

There she is, perched on her manger, looking over the
boards into the day
Like a belle at her window.
And immediately she sees me she blinks, stares, doesn't
know me, turns her head and ignores me vulgarly,
with a wooden blank on her face.

What do I care for her, the ugly female, standing up there
with her long tangled sides like an old rug thrown over
a fence.
But she puts her nose down shrewdly enough when the
knot is untied,
And jumps staccato to earth, a sharp, dry jump, still
ignoring me,
Pretending to look round the stall.

Come on, you crapa! I'm not your servant!

She turns her head away with an obtuse, female sort of
deafness, bête.
And then invariably she crouches her rear and makes water.
That being her way of answer, if I speak to her. –
    Self-conscious!
Le bestie non parlano, poverine!

She was bought at Giardini fair, on the sands, for six
hundred lire.

An obstinate old witch, almost jerking the rope from my
hands to eat the acanthus, or bite at the almond buds,
and make me wait.
Yet the moment I hate her she trips mild and smug like a
woman going to mass.
The moment I really detest her.

Queer it is, suddenly, in the garden
To catch sight of her standing like some huge, ghoulish
grey bird in the air, on the bough of the leaning
almond tree,
Straight as a board on the bough, looking down like some
hairy horrid God the Father in a William Blake
imagination.

Come down, crapa, out of that almond tree!

Instead of which she strangely rears on her perch in the
air, vast beast,
And strangely paws the air, delicate,
And reaches her black-striped face up like a snake, far up,
Subtly, to the twigs overhead, far up, vast beast,
And snaps them sharp, with a little twist of her anaconda
head;
All her great hairy-shaggy belly open against the morning.

At seasons she curls back her tail like a green leaf in the
fire,
Or like a lifted hand, hailing at her wrong end.
And having exposed the pink place of her nakedness,
fixedly,
She trots on blithe toes,
And if you look at her, she looks back with a cold, sardonic
stare.

Sardonic, sardonyx, rock of cold fire.
See me? she says, *That's me!*

That's her.

Then she leaps the rocks like a quick rock,
Her back-bone sharp as a rock,
Sheer will.
Along which ridge of libidinous magnetism
Defiant, curling the leaf of her tail as if she were curling her
    lip behind her at all life,
Libidinous desire runs back and forth, asserting itself in
    that little lifted bare hand.

Yet she has such adorable spurty kids, like spurts of black
    ink.
And in a month again is as if she had never had them.

And when the billy goat mounts her
She is brittle as brimstone.
While his slitted eyes squint back to the roots of his ears.

TAORMINA

ELEPHANT

You go down shade to the river, where naked men sit on
    flat brown rocks, to watch the ferry, in the sun;
And you cross the ferry with the naked people, go up the
    tropical lane
Through the palm-trees and past hollow paddy-fields
    where naked men are threshing rice
And the monolithic water-buffaloes, like old, muddy
    stones with hair on them, are being idle;
And through the shadow of bread-fruit trees, with their
    dark green, glossy, fanged leaves
Very handsome, and some pure yellow fanged leaves;
Out into the open, where the path runs on the top of a
    dyke between paddy-fields:

And there, of course, you meet a huge and mud-grey
    elephant advancing his frontal bone, his trunk curled
    round a log of wood:
So you step down the bank, to make way.

Shuffle, shuffle, and his little wicked eye has seen you as he
    advances above you,
The slow beast curiously spreading his round feet for the
    dust.
And the slim naked man slips down, and the beast deposits
    the lump of wood, carefully.
The keeper hooks the vast knee, the creature salaams.

White man, you are saluted.
Pay a few cents.

But the best is the Pera-hera, at midnight, under the
    tropical stars,
With a pale little wisp of a Prince of Wales, diffident, up in
    a small pagoda on the temple side
And white people in evening dress buzzing and crowding
    the stand upon the grass below and opposite:
And at last the Pera-hera procession, flambeaux aloft in the
    tropical night, of blazing cocoa-nut,
Naked dark men beneath,
And the huge frontal of three great elephants stepping
    forth to the tom-tom's beat, in the torch-light,
Slowly sailing in gorgeous apparel through the flame-
    light, in front of a towering, grimacing white image
    of wood.

The elephant bells striking slow, tong-tong, tong-tong,
To music and queer chanting:
Enormous shadow-processions filing on in the flare of fire
In the fume of cocoa-nut oil, in the sweating tropical night,
In the noise of the tom-toms and singers;

Elephants after elephants curl their trunks, vast shadows,
and some cry out
As they approach and salaam, under the dripping fire of
the torches
That pale fragment of a Prince up there, whose motto is
Ich dien.

Pale, dispirited Prince, with his chin on his hands, his
nerves tired out,
Watching and hardly seeing the trunk-curl approach and
clumsy, knee-lifting salaam
Of the hugest, oldest of beasts, in the night and the fire-
flare below.

He is royalty, pale and dejected fragment up aloft.
And down below huge homage of shadowy beasts, bare-
foot and trunk-lipped in the night.

Chieftains, three of them abreast, on foot
Strut like peg-tops, wound around with hundreds of yards
of fine linen.
They glimmer with tissue of gold, and golden threads on a
jacket of velvet,
And their faces are dark, and fat, and important.

They are royalty, dark-faced royalty, showing the conscious
whites of their eyes
And stepping in homage, stubborn, to that nervous pale
lad up there.

More elephants, tong, tong-tong, loom up,
Huge, more tassels swinging, more dripping fire of new
cocoa-nut cressets
High, high flambeaux, smoking of the east;
And scarlet hot embers of torches knocked out of the

sockets among bare feet of elephants and men on the
    path in the dark.
And devil dancers, luminous with sweat, dancing on to the
    shudder of drums,
Tom-toms, weird music of the devil, voices of men from
    the jungle singing;
Endless, under the Prince.

Towards the tail of the everlasting procession
In the long hot night, more dancers from insignificant
    villages,
And smaller, more frightened elephants.

Men-peasants from jungle villages dancing and running
    with sweat and laughing,
Naked dark men with ornaments on, on their naked arms
    and their naked breasts, the grooved loins
Gleaming like metal with running sweat as they suddenly
    turn, feet apart,
And dance and dance, forever dance, with breath half
    sobbing in dark, sweat-shining breasts,
And lustrous great tropical eyes unveiled now, gleaming a
    kind of laugh,
A naked, gleaming dark laugh, like a secret out in the dark,
And flare of a tropical energy, tireless, afire in the dark,
    slim limbs and breasts;
Perpetual, fire-laughing motion, among the slow shuffle
Of elephants,
The hot dark blood of itself a-laughing, wet, half-devilish,
    men all motion
Approaching under that small pavilion, and tropical eyes
    dilated look up
Inevitably look up
To the Prince,
To that tired remnant of royalty up there
Whose motto is *Ich dien.*

As if the homage of the kindled blood of the east
Went up in wavelets to him, from the breasts and eyes of
    jungle torch-men.
And he couldn't take it.

What would they do, those jungle men running with
    sweat, with the strange dark laugh in their eyes,
    glancing up,
And the sparse-haired elephants slowly following,
If they knew that his motto was *Ich dien?*
And that he meant it.

They begin to understand,
The rickshaw boys begin to understand;
And then the devil comes into their faces,
But a different sort, a cold, rebellious, jeering devil.

In elephants and the east are two devils, in all men maybe.
The mystery of the dark mountain of blood, reeking in
    homage, in lust, in rage,
And passive with everlasting patience;
Then the little, cunning pig-devil of the elephant's lurking
    eyes, the unbeliever.

We dodged, when the Pera-hera was finished, under the
    hanging, hairy pig's tails
And the flat, flaccid mountains of the elephants' standing
    haunches,
Vast-blooded beasts,
Myself so little dodging rather scared against the eternal
    wrinkled pillars of their legs, as they were being
    dismantled;
Then I knew they were dejected, having come to hear the
    repeated
Royal summons: *Dient Ihr!*
Serve!

Serve, vast mountainous blood, in submission and splendour, serve royalty.

Instead of which, the silent, fatal emission from that pale shattered boy up there:

Ich dien.

That's why the night fell in frustration.

That's why, as the elephants ponderously, with unseeming swiftness galloped uphill in the night, going back to the jungle villages,

As the elephant bells sounded tong-tong-tong, bell of the temple of blood, in the night, swift-striking,

And the crowd like a field of rice in the dark gave way like liquid to the dark

Looming gallop of the beasts,

It was as if the great bare bulks of elephants in the obscure light went over the hill-brow swiftly, with their tails between their legs, in haste to get away,

Their bells sounding frustrate and sinister.

And all the dark-faced, cotton-wrapped people, more numerous and whispering than grains of rice in a rice-field at night,

All the dark-faced, cotton-wrapped people, a countless host on the shores of the lake, like thick wild rice by the water's edge,

Waiting for the fireworks of the after-show,

As the rockets went up, and the glare passed over countless faces, dark as black rice growing,

Showing a glint of teeth, and glancing tropical eyes aroused in the night,

There was the faintest twist of mockery in every face, across the hiss of wonders as the rocket burst

High, high up, in flakes, shimmering flakes of blue fire, above the palm trees of the islet in the lake.

O faces upturned to the glare, O tropical wonder, wonder,
    a miracle in heaven!
And the shadow of a jeer, of underneath disappointment,
    as the rocket-coruscation died, and shadow was the
    same as before.

They were foiled, the myriad whispering dark-faced cotton-
    wrapped people.
They had come to see royalty,
To bow before royalty, in the land of elephants, bow deep,
    bow deep.
Bow deep, for it's good as a draught of cool water to bow
    very, very low to the royal.

And all there was to bow to, a weary, diffident boy whose
    motto is *Ich dien*.
I serve! I serve! in all the weary irony of his mien – *'Tis I
    who serve!*
Drudge to the public.

I wish they had given the three feathers to me;
That I had been he in the pavilion, as in a pepper-box aloft
    and alone
To stand and hold feathers, three feathers above the world,
And say to them: *Dient Ihr! Dient!*
Omnes, vos omnes, servite.
Serve me, I am meet to be served.
Being royal of the gods.

And to the elephants:
First great beasts of the earth
A prince has come back to you,
Blood-mountains.
Crook the knee and be glad.

KANDY

176

KANGAROO

In the northern hemisphere
Life seems to leap at the air, or skim under the wind
Like stags on rocky ground, or pawing horses, or springy
     scut-tailed rabbits.

Or else rush horizontal to charge at the sky's horizon,
Like bulls or bisons or wild pigs.

Or slip like water slippery towards its ends,
As foxes, stoats, and wolves, and prairie dogs.

Only mice, and moles, and rats, and badgers, and beavers,
     and perhaps bears
Seem belly-plumbed to the earth's mid-navel.
Or frogs that when they leap come flop, and flop to the
     centre of the earth.

But the yellow antipodal Kangaroo, when she sits up
Who can unseat her, like a liquid drop that is heavy, and
     just touches earth.

The downward drip.
The down-urge.
So much denser than cold-blooded frogs.

Delicate mother Kangaroo
Sitting up there rabbit-wise, but huge, plumb-weighted,
And lifting her beautiful slender face, oh! so much more
     gently and finely-lined than a rabbit's, or than a hare's,
Lifting her face to nibble at a round white peppermint
     drop, which she loves, sensitive mother Kangaroo.

Her sensitive, long, pure-bred face.
Her full antipodal eyes, so dark,
So big and quiet and remote, having watched so many
     empty dawns in silent Australia.

Her little loose hands, and drooping Victorian shoulders.
And then her great weight below the waist, her vast pale
belly
With a thin young yellow little paw hanging out, and
straggle of a long thin ear, like ribbon,
Like a funny trimming to the middle of her belly, thin
little dangle of an immature paw, and one thin ear.

Her belly, her big haunches
And in addition, the great muscular python-stretch of her
tail.

There, she shan't have any more peppermint drops.
So she wistfully, sensitively sniffs the air, and then turns,
goes off in slow sad leaps
On the long flat skis of her legs,
Steered and propelled by that steel-strong snake of a tail.

Stops again, half turns, inquisitive to look back.
While something stirs quickly in her belly, and a lean little
face comes out, as from a window,
Peaked and a bit dismayed,
Only to disappear again quickly away from the sight of the
world, to snuggle down in the warmth,
Leaving the trail of a different paw hanging out.

Still she watches with eternal, cocked wistfulness!
How full her eyes are, like the full, fathomless, shining eyes
of an Australian black-boy
Who has been lost so many centuries on the margins of
existence!

She watches with insatiable wistfulness.
Untold centuries of watching for something to come,
For a new signal from life, in that silent lost land of the
South.

Where nothing bites but insects and snakes and the sun,
small life.
Where no bull roared, no cow ever lowed, no stag cried,
no leopard screeched, no lion coughed, no dog
barked,
But all was silent save for parrots occasionally, in the
haunted blue bush.

Wistfully watching, with wonderful liquid eyes.
And all her weight, all her blood, dripping sack-wise down
towards the earth's centre,
And the live little one taking in its paw at the door of her
belly.

Leap then, and come down on the line that draws to the
earth's deep, heavy centre.

SYDNEY

BIBBLES

BIBBLES
Little black dog in New Mexico,
Little black snub-nosed bitch with a shoved-out jaw
And a wrinkled reproachful look;
Little black female pup, sort of French bull, they say,
With bits of brindle coming through, like rust, to show
you're not pure;
Not pure, Bibbles,
Bibsey, bat-eared dog;
Not black enough!

First live thing I've 'owned' since the lop-eared rabbits
when I was a lad,
And those over-prolific white mice, and Adolf, and Rex
whom I didn't own.
And even now, Bibbles, little Ma'am, it's you who
appropriated me, not I you.

As Benjamin Franklin appropriated Providence to his
    purposes.

Oh Bibbles, black little bitch
I'd never have let you appropriate me, had I known.
I never dreamed, till now, of the awful time the Lord must
    have, 'owning' humanity,
Especially democratic live-by-love humanity.

Oh Bibbles, oh Pips, oh Pipsey
You little black love-bird!
Don't you love *everybody*!!!
Just everybody.
You love 'em all.
Believe in the One Identity, don't you,
You little Walt-Whitmanesque bitch?

First time I lost you in Taos plaza
And found you after endless chasing,
Came upon you prancing round the corner in exuberant,
    bibbling affection
After the black-green skirts of a yellow-green old Mexican
    woman
Who hated you, and kept looking round at you and cursing
    you in a mutter,
While you pranced and bounced with love of her, you
    indiscriminating animal,
All your wrinkled *miserere* Chinese black little face beaming
And your black little body bouncing and wriggling
With indiscriminate love, Bibbles;
I had a moment's pure detestation of you.
As I rushed like an idiot round the corner after you
Yelling: *Pips! Pips! Bibbles!*

I've had moments of hatred of you since,
Loving everybody!
'To you, whoever you are, with endless embrace!' –

That's you, Pipsey,
With your imbecile bit of a tail in a love-flutter.
You omnipip.

Not that you're merely a softy, oh dear me no,
You know which side your bread is buttered.
You don't care a rap for anybody.
But you love lying warm between warm human thighs,
    indiscriminate,
And you love to make somebody love you, indiscriminate,
You love to lap up affection, to wallow in it,
And then turn tail to the next comer, for a new dollop.

And start prancing and licking and cuddling again, in-
    discriminate.

Oh yes, I know your little game.

Yet you're so nice,
So quick, like a little black dragon.
So fierce, when the coyotes howl, barking back like a whole
    little lion, and rumbling,
And starting forward in the dusk, with your little black fur
    all bristling like plush
Against those coyotes, who would swallow you like an
    oyster.

And in the morning, when the bedroom door is opened,
Rushing in like a little black whirlwind, leaping straight as
    an arrow on the bed at the pillow
And turning the day suddenly into a black tornado of *joie
    de vivre*, Chinese dragon.

So funny
Lobbing wildly through deep snow like a rabbit,
Hurtling like a black ball through the snow,
Champing it, tossing a mouthful,
Little black spot in the landscape!

So absurd

Pelting behind on the dusty trail when the horse sets off
      home at a gallop:

Left in the dust behind like a dust-ball tearing along

Coming up on fierce little legs, tearing fast to catch up, a
      real little dust-pig, ears almost blown away,

And black eyes bulging bright in a dust-mask

Chinese-dragon-wrinkled, with a pink mouth grinning,
      under jaw shoved out

And white teeth showing in your dragon-grin as you race,
      you split-face,

Like a trundling projectile swiftly whirling up,

Cocking your eyes at me as you come alongside, to see if
      I'm I on the horse,

And panting with that split grin,

All your game little body dust-smooth like a little pig, poor
      Pips.

Plenty of game old spirit in you, Bibbles.

Plenty of game old spunk, little bitch.

How you hate being brushed with the boot-brush, to
      brush all that dust out of your wrinkled face,

Don't you?

How you hate being made to look undignified, Ma'am;

How you hate being laughed at, Miss Superb!

Blackberry face!

Plenty of conceit in you.

Unblemished belief in your own perfection

And utter lovableness, you ugly-mug;

Chinese puzzle-face,

Wrinkled underhung physog that looks as if it had done
      with everything,

Through with everything.

Instead of which you sit there and roll your head like a
    canary
And show a tiny bunch of white teeth in your underhung
    blackness,
Self-conscious little bitch,
Aiming again at being loved.

Let the merest scallywag come to the door and you leap
    your very dearest love at him,
As if now, at last, here was the one you *finally* loved,
Finally loved;
And even the dirtiest scallywag is taken in,
Thinking: *This dog sure has taken a fancy to me.*

You miserable little bitch of love-tricks,
I know your game.

Me or the Mexican who comes to chop wood
All the same,
All humanity is jam to you.

Everybody so dear, and yourself so ultra-beloved
That you have to run out at last and eat filth,
Gobble up filth, you horror, swallow utter abomination
    and fresh-dropped dung.

You stinker.
You worse than a carrion-crow.
Reeking dung-mouth.
You love-bird.

Reject nothing, sings Walt Whitman.
So you, you go out at last and eat the unmentionable,
In your appetite for affection.

And then you run in to vomit it in my house!
I get my love back.
And I have to clean up after you, filth which even blind
    Nature rejects

From the pit of your stomach;
But you, you snout-face, you reject nothing, you merge so
much in love
You must eat even that.

Then when I dust you a bit with a juniper twig
You run straight away to live with somebody else,
Fawn before them, and love them as if they were the ones
you had *really* loved all along.
And they're taken in.
They feel quite tender over you, till you play the same trick
on them, dirty bitch.

Fidelity! Loyalty! Attachment!
Oh, these are abstractions to your nasty little belly.
You must always be a-waggle with LOVE.
Such a waggle of love you can hardly distinguish one
human from another.
You love one after another, on one condition, that each
one loves *you* most.
Democratic little bull-bitch, dirt-eating little swine.

But now, my lass, you've got your Nemesis on your track,
Now you've come sex-alive, and the great ranch dogs are
all after you.
They're after what they can get, and don't you turn tail!
You loved 'em all so much before, didn't you, loved 'em
indiscriminate?
You don't love 'em now.
They want something of you, so you squeak and come
pelting indoors.

Come pelting to me, now the other folk have found you
out, and the dogs are after you.
Oh yes, you're found out. I heard them kick you out of the
ranch house:
Get out, you little, soft fool!!

And didn't you turn your eyes up at me then?
And didn't you cringe on the floor like any inkspot!
And crawl away like a black snail!
And doesn't everybody loathe you then!
And aren't your feelings violated, you high-bred little
    love-bitch!

For you're sensitive,
In many ways very finely bred.
But bred in conceit that the world is all for love
Of you, my bitch: till you get so far you eat filth.
Fool, in spite of your pretty ways, and quaint, know-all,
    wrinkled old aunty's face.

So now, what with great Airedale dogs,
And a kick or two,
And a few vomiting bouts,
And a juniper switch,
You look at me for discrimination, don't you?
Look up at me with misgiving in your bulging eyes,
And fear in the smoky whites of your eyes, you nigger;
And you're puzzled,
You think you'd better mind your P's and Q's for a bit,
Your sensitive love-pride being all hurt.

All right, my little bitch.
You learn loyalty rather than loving,
And I'll protect you.

                                       LOBO

MOUNTAIN LION

CLIMBING through the January snow, into the Lobo
    canyon
Dark grow the spruce trees, blue is the balsam, water
    sounds still unfrozen, and the trail is still evident.

Men!
Two men!
Men! The only animal in the world to fear!

They hesitate.
We hesitate.
They have a gun.
We have no gun.

Then we all advance, to meet.

Two Mexicans, strangers, emerging out of the dark and
    snow and inwardness of the Lobo valley.
What are they doing here on this vanishing trail?

What is he carrying?
Something yellow.
A deer?

Qué tiene, amigo? —
León —

He smiles, foolishly, as if he were caught doing wrong.
And we smile, foolishly, as if we didn't know.
He is quite gentle and dark-faced.

It is a mountain lion,
A long, slim cat, yellow like a lioness.
Dead.

He trapped her this morning, he says, smiling foolishly.

Lift up her face,
Her round, bright face, bright as frost.
Her round, fine-fashioned head, with two dead ears:
And stripes in the brilliant frost of her face, sharp, fine
    dark rays,
Dark, keen, fine rays in the brilliant frost of her face.
Beautiful dead eyes.

They go out towards the open;
We go on into the gloom of Lobo.

And above the trees I found her lair,
A hole in the blood-orange brilliant rocks that stick up, a
    little cave.
And bones, and twigs, and a perilous ascent.

So, she will never leap up that way again, with the yellow
    flash of a mountain lion's long shoot!
And her bright striped frost-face will never watch any
    more, out of the shadow of the cave in the blood-
    orange rock,
Above the trees of the Lobo dark valley-mouth!

Instead, I look out.
And out to the dim of the desert, like a dream, never real;
To the snow of the Sangre de Cristo mountains, the ice of
    the mountains of Picoris,
And near across at the opposite steep of snow, green trees
    motionless standing in snow, like a Christmas toy.

And I think in this empty world there was room for me
    and a mountain lion.
And I think in the world beyond, how easily we might
    spare a million or two of humans
And never miss them.
Yet what a gap in the world, the missing white frost-face
    of that slim yellow mountain lion!

LOBO

THE RED WOLF

OVER the heart of the west, the Taos desert
Circles an eagle,
And it's dark between me and him.

187

The sun, as he waits a moment, huge and liquid
Standing without feet on the rim of the far-off mesa
Says: *Look for a last long time then! Look! Look well! I am*
     going.
So he pauses and is beholden, and straightway is gone.

And the Indian, in a white sheet
Wrapped to the eyes, the sheet bound close on his brows,
Stands saying: *See, I'm invisible!*
Behold how you can't behold me!
The invisible in its shroud!

Now that the sun has gone, and the aspen leaves
And the cotton-wood leaves are fallen, as good as fallen,
And the ponies are in corral,
And it's night:
Why, more has gone than all these;
And something has come.
A red wolf stands on the shadow's dark red rim.

Day has gone to dust on the sage-grey desert
Like a white Christus fallen to dust from a cross;
To dust, to ash, on the twilit floor of the desert.
And a black crucifix like a dead tree spreading wings;
Maybe a black eagle with its wings out
Left lonely in the night
In a sort of worship.

And coming down upon us, out of the dark concave
Of the eagle's wings,
And the coffin-like slit where the Indian's eyes are,
And the absence of cotton-wood leaves, or of aspen,
Even the absence of dark-crossed donkeys:
Come tall old demons, smiling
The Indian smile,
Saying: *How do you do, you pale-face?*

I am very well, old demon.
How are you?

Call me Harry if you will,
Call me Old Harry, says he.
Or the abbreviation of Nicolas,
Nick, Old Nick, maybe.

Well, you're a dark old demon,
And I'm a pale-face like a homeless dog
That has followed the sun from the dawn through the east
Trotting east and east and east till the sun himself went
    home,
And left me homeless here in the dark at your door.
How do you think we'll get on,
Old demon, you and I?

You and I, you pale-face,
Pale-face you and I
Don't get on.

Mightn't we try?

Where's your God, you white one?
Where's your white God?

He fell to dust as the twilight fell,
Was fume as I trod
The last step out of the east.

Then you're a lost white dog of a pale-face,
And the day's now dead . . .

Touch me carefully, old father,
My beard is red.

Thin red wolf of a pale-face,
Thin red wolf, go home.

I have no home, old father.
That's why I come.

We take no hungry stray from the pale-face . . .

Father, you are not asked.
I am come. I am here. The red-dawn-wolf
Sniffs round your place.
Lifts up his voice and howls to the walls of the pueblo,
Announcing he's here.

The dogs of the dark pueblo
Have long fangs . . .

Has the red wolf trotted east and east and east,
From the far, far other end of the day
To fear a few fangs?

Across the pueblo river
That dark old demon and I
Thus say a few words to each other.

And wolf, he calls me, and red.
I call him no names.
He says, however, he is Star-Road.
I say, he can go back the same gait.

As for me . . .
Since I trotted at the tail of the sun as far as ever the
    creature went west,
And lost him here,
I'm going to sit down on my tail right here
And wait for him to come back with a new story.
I'm the red wolf, says the dark old father.
All right, the red dawn wolf I am.

TAOS

Pansies

TWO PERFORMING ELEPHANTS

He stands with his forefeet on the drum
and the other, the old one, the pallid hoary female
must creep her great bulk beneath the bridge of him.

On her knees, in utmost caution
all agog, and curling up her trunk
she edges through without upsetting him.
Triumph! the ancient pig-tailed monster!

When her trick is to climb over him
with what shadow-like slow carefulness
she skims him, sensitive
as shadows from the ages gone and perished
in touching him, and planting her round feet.

While the wispy, modern children, half-afraid
watch silent. The looming of the hoary, far-gone ages
is too much for them.

NATURAL COMPLEXION

But, you see, said the handsome young man with the
      chamois gloves
to the woman rather older than himself,
if you don't use rouge and a lip-stick, in Paris,
they'll take you for a woman of the people.

So spoke the British gentleman
pulling on his chamois gloves
and using his most melodious would-be-Oxford voice.

And the woman said: Dear me!
how rough that would be on you, darling!

Only, if you insist on pulling on those chamois gloves
I swear I'll pull off my knickers, right in the Rue de la
    Paix.

THE OXFORD VOICE

WHEN you hear it languishing
and hooing and cooing and sidling through the front teeth,
        the Oxford voice
        or worse still
        the would-be-Oxford voice
you don't even laugh any more, you can't.

For every blooming bird is an Oxford cuckoo nowadays,
you can't sit on a bus nor in the tube
but it breathes gently and languishingly in the back of your
    neck.

And oh, so seductively superior, so seductively
        self-effacingly
        deprecatingly
        superior. —

We wouldn't insist on it for a moment
        but we are
        we are
        you admit we are
        superior. —

SWAN

FAR-OFF
at the core of space
at the quick of time

beats
and goes still
the great swan upon the waters of all endings
the swan within vast chaos, within the electron.

For us
no longer he swims calmly
nor clacks the forces furrowing a great gay trail
of happy energy,
nor is he nesting passive upon the atoms,
nor flying north desolative icewards
to the sleep of ice,
nor feeding in the marshes,
nor honking horn-like into the twilight. —

But he stoops, now
in the dark
upon us;
he is treading our women
and we men are put out
as the vast white bird
furrows our featherless women
with unknown shocks
and stamps his black marsh-feet on their white and marshy
    flesh.

LEDA

COME not with kisses
not with caresses
of hands and lips and murmurings;
come with a hiss of wings
and sea-touch tip of a beak
and treading of wet, webbed, wave-working feet
into the marsh-soft belly.

GIVE us gods, Oh give them us!
Give us gods.
We are so tired of men
and motor-power. –

But not gods grey-bearded and dictatorial,
nor yet that pale young man afraid of fatherhood
shelving substance on to the woman, Madonna mia!
    shabby virgin!
nor gusty Jove, with his eye on immortal tarts,
nor even the musical, suave young fellow
wooing boys and beauty.

Give us gods
give us something else –

Beyond the great bull that bellowed through space, and
    got his throat cut.
Beyond even that eagle, that phœnix, hanging over the
    gold egg of all things,
further still, before the curled horns of the ram stepped
    forth
or the stout swart beetle rolled the globe of dung in which
    man should hatch,
or even the sly gold serpent fatherly lifted his head off the
    earth to think –

Give us gods before these –
Thou shalt have other gods before these.

Where the waters end in marshes
swims the wild swan
sweeps the high goose above the mists
honking in the gloom the honk of procreation from such
    throats.

Mists
where the electron behaves and misbehaves as it will,
where the forces tie themselves up into knots of atoms
and come untied;

mists
of mistiness complicated into knots and clots that barge
    about
and bump on one another and explode into more mist, or
    don't,
mist of energy most scientific –
But give us gods!

Look then
where the father of all things swims in a mist of atoms
electrons and energies, quantums and relativities
mists, wreathing mists,
like a wild swan, or a goose, whose honk goes through
    my bladder.
And in the dark unscientific I feel the drum-winds of his
    wings
and the drip of his cold, webbed feet, mud-black
brush over my face as he goes
to seek the women in the dark, our women, our weird
    women whom he treads
with dreams and thrusts that make them cry in their sleep.

Gods, do you ask for gods?
Where there is woman there is swan.

Do you think, scientific man, you'll be father of your own
    babies?
Don't imagine it.
There'll be babies born that are cygnets, O my soul!
young wild swans!
And babies of women will come out young wild geese, O
    my heart!
the geese that saved Rome, and will lose London.

WON'T IT BE STRANGE — ?

Won't it be strange, when the nurse brings the new-born
    infant
to the proud father, and shows its little, webbed greenish
    feet

made to smite the waters behind it?
or the round, wild vivid eye of a wild-goose staring
out of fathomless skies and seas?
or when it utters that undaunted little bird-cry
of one who will settle on ice-bergs, and honk across the
    Nile? —

And when the father says: This is none of mine!
Woman, where got you this little beast? —
will there be a whistle of wings in the air, and an icy
    draught?
will the singing of swans, high up, high up, invisible
break the drums of his ears
and leave him forever listening for the answer?

WHEN I WENT TO THE CIRCUS

When I went to the circus that had pitched on the waste
    lot
it was full of uneasy people
frightened of the bare earth and the temporary canvas
and the smell of horses and other beasts
instead of merely the smell of man.

Monkeys rode rather grey and wizened
on curly plump piebald ponies
and the children uttered a little cry —
and dogs jumped through hoops and turned somersaults

and then the geese scuttled in in a little flock
and round the ring they went to the sound of the whip
then doubled, and back, with a funny up-flutter of wings –
and the children suddenly shouted out.

Then came the hush again, like a hush of fear.

The tight-rope lady, pink and blonde and nude-looking,
    with a few gold spangles
footed cautiously out on the rope, turned prettily, spun
    round
bowed, and lifted her foot in her hand, smiled, swung her
    parasol
to another balance, tripped round, poised, and slowly sank
her handsome thighs down, down, till she slept her splen-
    did body on the rope.
When she rose, tilting her parasol, and smiled at the cautious
    people
they cheered, but nervously.

The trapeze man, slim and beautiful and like a fish in the
    air
swung great curves through the upper space, and came
    down like a star.
– And the people applauded, with hollow, frightened
    applause.

The elephants, huge and grey, loomed their curved bulk
    through the dusk
and sat up, taking strange postures, showing the pink soles
    of their feet
and curling their precious live trunks like ammonites
and moving always with soft slow precision
as when a great ship moves to anchor.
The people watched and wondered, and seemed to resent
    the mystery that lies in beasts.

Horses, gay horses, swirling round and plaiting
in a long line, their heads laid over each other's necks;
they were happy, they enjoyed it;
all the creatures seemed to enjoy the game
in the circus, with their circus people.

But the audience, compelled to wonder
compelled to admire the bright rhythms of moving bodies
compelled to see the delicate skill of flickering human
    bodies
flesh flamey and a little heroic, even in a tumbling clown,
they were not really happy.
There was no gushing response, as there is at the film.

When modern people see the carnal body dauntless and
    flickering gay
playing among the elements neatly, beyond competition
and displaying no personality,
modern people are depressed.

Modern people feel themselves at a disadvantage.
They know they have no bodies that could play among the
    elements.
They have only their personalities, that are best seen flat,
    on the film,
flat personalities in two dimensions, imponderable and
    touchless.

And they grudge the circus people the swooping gay
    weight of limbs
that flower in mere movement,
and they grudge them the immediate, physical understand-
    ing they have with their circus beasts,
and they grudge them their circus life altogether.

Yet the strange, almost frightened shout of delight that
    comes now and then from the children

shows that the children vaguely know how cheated they
    are of their birthright
in the bright wild circus flesh.

WHATEVER MAN MAKES

WHATEVER man makes and makes it live
lives because of the life put into it.
A yard of India muslin is alive with Hindu life.
And a Navajo woman, weaving her rug in the pattern of
    her dream
must run the pattern out in a little break at the end
so that her soul can come out, back to her.

But in the odd pattern, like snake-marks on the sand
it leaves its trail.

THE ELEPHANT IS SLOW TO MATE

THE elephant, the huge old beast,
    is slow to mate;
he finds a female, they show no haste
    they wait

for the sympathy in their vast shy hearts
    slowly, slowly to rouse
as they loiter along the river-beds
    and drink and browse

and dash in a panic through the brake
    of forest with the herd,
and sleep in massive silence, and wake
    together without a word.

So slowly the great hot elephant hearts
    grow full of desire,
and the great beasts mate in secret at last,
    hiding their fire.

Oldest they are and the wisest of beasts
    so they know at last
how to wait for the loneliest of feasts
    for the full repast.

They do not snatch, they do not tear;
    their massive blood
moves as the moon-tides, near, more near
    till they touch in flood.

THE GAZELLE CALF

THE gazelle calf, O my children,
goes behind its mother across the desert,
goes behind its mother on blithe bare foot
requiring no shoes, O my children!

THE MOSQUITO KNOWS

THE mosquito knows full well, small as he is
he's a beast of prey.
But after all
he only takes his bellyful,
he doesn't put my blood in the bank.

FIDELITY

FIDELITY and love are two different things, like a flower
    and a gem.
And love, like a flower, will fade, will change into some-
    thing else
or it would not be flowery.

O flowers they fade because they are moving swiftly; a
    little torrent of life

leaps up to the summit of the stem, gleams, turns over
    round the bend
of the parabola of curved flight,
sinks, and is gone, like a comet curving into the invisible.

O flowers, they are all the time travelling
like comets, and they come into our ken
for a day, for two days, and withdraw, slowly vanish again.

And we, we must take them on the wing, and let them go.
Embalmed flowers are not flowers, immortelles are not
    flowers;
flowers are just a motion, a swift motion, a coloured ges-
    ture;
that is their loveliness. And that is love.

But a gem is different. It lasts so much longer than we do
so much much much much longer
that it seems to last for ever.
Yet we know it is flowing away
as flowers are, and we are, only slower.
The wonderful slow flowing of the sapphire!

All flows, and every flow is related to every other flow.
Flowers and sapphires and us, diversely streaming.

In the old days, when sapphires were breathed upon and
    brought forth
during the wild orgasms of chaos
time was much slower, when the rocks came forth.
It took aeons to make a sapphire, aeons for it to pass away.

And a flower it takes a summer.

And man and woman are like the earth, that brings forth
    flowers
in summer, and love, but underneath is rock.

Older than flowers, older than ferns, older than foramini-
　　feræ,
older than plasm altogether is the soul of a man under-
　　neath.

And when, throughout all the wild orgasms of love
slowly a gem forms, in the ancient, once-more-molten
　　rocks
of two human hearts, two ancient rocks, a man's heart and
　　a woman's,
that is the crystal of peace, the slow hard jewel of trust,
the sapphire of fidelity.
The gem of mutual peace emerging from the wild chaos of
　　love.

NOTTINGHAM'S NEW UNIVERSITY

In Nottingham, that dismal town
where I went to school and college,
they've built a new university
for a new dispensation of knowledge.

Built it most grand and cakeily
out of the noble loot
derived from shrewd cash-chemistry
by good Sir Jesse Boot.

Little I thought, when I was a lad
and turned my modest penny
over on Boot's Cash-Chemist's counter,
that Jesse, by turning many

millions of similar honest pence
over, would make a pile
that would rise at last and blossom out
in grand and cakey style

into a university
where smart men would dispense
doses of smart cash-chemistry
in language of common-sense!

That future Nottingham lads would be
cash-chemically B.Sc.
that Nottingham lights would rise and say:
– By Boots I am M.A.

From this I learn, though I knew it before
that culture has her roots
in the deep dung of cash, and lore
is a last offshoot of Boots.

NO! MR LAWRENCE!

No, Mr Lawrence, it's not like that!
I don't mind telling you
I know a thing or two about love,
perhaps more than you do.

And what I know is that you make it
too nice, too beautiful.
It's not like that, you know; you fake it.
It's really rather dull.

RED-HERRING

My father was a working man
    and a collier was he,
at six in the morning they turned him down
    and they turned him up for tea.

My mother was a superior soul
    a superior soul was she,

cut out to play a superior role
 in the god-damn bourgeoisie.

We children were the in-betweens
 little non-descripts were we,
indoors we called each other *you*,
 outside, it was *tha* and *thee*.

But time has fled, our parents are dead,
 we've risen in the world all three;
but still we are in-betweens, we tread
 between the devil and the deep sad sea.

I am a member of the bourgeoisie
 and a servant-maid brings me my tea –
But I'm always longing for someone to say
 'ark 'ere, lad! atween thee an' me

they're a' a b – – – d – lot o' – – – s,
 an' I reckon it's nowt but right
we should start an' kick their – – ses for 'em
 an' tell 'em to – – – – –.

TO WOMEN, AS FAR AS I'M CONCERNED

THE feelings I don't have, I don't have.
The feelings I don't have, I won't say I have.
The feelings you say you have, you don't have.
The feelings you would like us both to have, we neither of
 us have.

The feelings people ought to have, they never have.
If people say they've got feelings, you may be pretty sure
 they haven't got them.

So if you want either of us to feel anything at all
you'd better abandon all idea of feelings altogether.

DESIRE IS DEAD

DESIRE may be dead
and still a man can be
a meeting place for sun and rain
wonder outwaiting pain
as in a wintry tree.

FIRE

FIRE is dearer to us than love or food,
hot, hurrying, yet it burns if you touch it.

What we ought to do
is not to add our love together, or our goodwill, or any of
    that,
for we're sure to bring in a lot of lies,
but our fire, our elemental fire
so that it rushes up in a huge blaze like a phallus into hollow
    space
and fecundates the zenith and the nadir
and sends off millions of sparks of new atoms
and singes us, and burns the house down.

NEMESIS

THE nemesis that awaits our civilisation
is social insanity
which in the end is always homicidal.

Sanity means the wholeness of the consciousness.
And our society is only part conscious, like an idiot.

If we do not rapidly open all the doors of consciousness
and freshen the putrid little space in which we are cribbed
the sky-blue walls of our unventilated heaven
will be bright red with blood.

WAGES

THE wages of work is cash.
The wages of cash is want more cash.
The wages of want more cash is vicious competition.
The wages of vicious competition is – the world we live in.

The work-cash-want circle is the viciousest circle
that ever turned men into fiends.

Earning a wage is a prison occupation
and a wage-earner is a sort of gaol-bird.

Earning a salary is a prison overseer's job
a gaoler instead of a gaol-bird.

Living on our income is strolling grandly outside the
    prison
in terror lest you have to go in. And since the work-prison
    covers
almost every scrap of the living earth, you stroll up and
    down
on a narrow beat, about the same as a prisoner taking
    exercise.

This is called universal freedom.

SELF-PROTECTION

WHEN science starts to be interpretive
it is more unscientific even than mysticism.

To make self-preservation and self-protection the first law
    of existence
is about as scientific as making suicide the first law of
    existence,
and amounts to very much the same thing.

A nightingale singing at the top of his voice
is neither hiding himself nor preserving himself nor pro-
    pagating his species;
he is giving himself away in every sense of the word;
and obviously, it is the culminating point of his existence.

A tiger is striped and golden for his own glory.
He would certainly be much more invisible if he were grey-
    green.

And I don't suppose the ichthyosaurus sparkled like the
    humming-bird,
no doubt he was khaki-coloured with muddy protective
    coloration,
so why didn't he survive?

As a matter of fact, the only creatures that seem to survive
are those that give themselves away in flash and sparkle
and gay flicker of joyful life;
those that go glittering abroad
with a bit of splendour.

Even mice play quite beautifully at shadows,
and some of them are brilliantly piebald.

I expect the dodo looked like a clod,
a drab and dingy bird.

LIZARD

A LIZARD ran out on a rock and looked up, listening
no doubt to the sounding of the spheres.
And what a dandy fellow! the right toss of a chin for you
and swirl of a tail!

If men were as much men as lizards are lizards
they'd be worth looking at.

RELATIVITY

I LIKE relativity and quantum theories
because I don't understand them
and they make me feel as if space shifted about like a swan
    that can't settle,
refusing to sit still and be measured;
and as if the atom were an impulsive thing
always changing its mind.

WHAT AILS THEE?

WHAT ails thee then, woman, what ails thee?
doesn't ter know?

If tha canna say't, come then an' scraight it out on my
    bosom!
Eh? – Men doesna ha'e bosoms? 'appen not, on'y tha
    knows what I mean.
Come then, tha can scraight it out on my shirt-front an'
    tha'lt feel better.

  – In the first place, I don't scraight.
And if I did, I certainly couldn't *scraight it out*.
And if I could, the last place I should choose
would be your shirt-front
or your manly bosom either.
So leave off trying putting the Robbie Burns touch over
  me
and kindly hand me the cigarettes
if you haven't smoked them all,
which you're much more likely to do
than to shelter anybody from the cau-auld blast.

CONUNDRUMS

TELL me a word
that you've often heard,
yet it makes you squint
if you see it in print!

Tell me a thing
that you've often seen,
yet if put in a book
it makes you turn green!

Tell me a thing
that you often do,
which, described in a story
shocks you through and through!

Tell me what's wrong
with words or with you
that you don't mind the thing
yet the name is taboo.

WILLY WET-LEG

I CAN'T stand Willy wet-leg,
can't stand him at any price.
He's resigned, and when you hit him
he lets you hit him twice.

Nettles and *More Pansies*

ANDRAITX – POMEGRANATE FLOWERS

It is June, it is June
the pomegranates are in flower,
the peasants are bending cutting the bearded wheat.

The pomegranates are in flower
beside the high road, past the deathly dust,
and even the sea is silent in the sun.

Short gasps of flame in the green of night, way off
the pomegranates are in flower,
small sharp red fires in the night of leaves.

And noon is suddenly dark, is lustrous, is silent and dark
men are unseen, beneath the shading hats;
only, from out the foliage of the secret loins
red flamelets here and there reveal
a man, a woman there.

THE HEART OF MAN

There is the other universe, of the heart of man
that we know nothing of, that we dare not explore.

A strange grey distance separates
our pale mind still from the pulsing continent
of the heart of man.

Fore-runners have barely landed on the shore
and no man knows, no woman knows
the mystery of the interior
when darker still than Congo or Amazon
flow the heart's rivers of fulness, desire and distress.

MORAL CLOTHING

When I am clothed I am a moral man,
and unclothed, the word has no meaning for me.

When I put on my coat, my coat has pockets
and in the pockets are things I require,
so I wish no man to pick my pocket
and I will pick the pocket of no man.

A man's business is one of his pockets, his bank account too
his credit, his name, his wife even may be just another of
    his pockets.
And I loathe the thought of being a pilferer
a pick-pocket.
That is why business seems to me despicable,
and most love-affairs, just sneak-thief pocket-picking
of dressed-up people.

When I stand in my shirt I have no pockets
therefore no morality of pockets;
but still my nakedness is clothed with responsibility
towards those near and dear to me, my very next of kin.
I am not yet alone.

Only when I am stripped stark naked I am alone
and without morals, and without immorality.
The invisible gods have no moral truck with us.

And if stark naked I approach a fellow-man or fellow-
    woman
they must be naked too,
and none of us must expect morality of each other:
I am that I am, take it or leave it.
Offer me nothing but that which you are, stark and strange.
Let there be no accommodation at this issue.

THE CHURCH

IF I was a member of the Church of Rome
I should advocate reform:
the marriage of priests
the priests to wear rose-colour or magenta in the streets
to teach the Resurrection in the flesh
to start the year on Easter Sunday
to add the mystery of Joy-in-Resurrection to the Mass
to inculcate the new conception of the Risen Man.

IN A SPANISH TRAM-CAR

SHE fanned herself with a violet fan
and looked sulky, under her thick straight brows.

The wisp of modern black mantilla
made her half Madonna, half Astarte.

Suddenly her yellow-brown eyes looked with a flare into
mine.
– We could sin together! –

The spark fell and kindled instantly on my blood,
then died out almost as swiftly.

She can keep her sin
She can sin with some thick-set Spaniard.
Sin doesn't interest me.

BELLS

THE Mohammedans say that the sound of bells
especially big ones, is obscene,

That hard clapper striking in a hard mouth
and resounding after with a long hiss of insistence
is obscene.

Yet bells call the Christians to God
especially clapper bells, hard tongues wagging in hard
    mouths,
metal hitting on metal, to enforce our attention . . .
and bring us to God.

The soft thudding of drums
of fingers or fists or soft-skinned sticks upon the stretched
    membrane of sound
sends summons in the old hollows of the sun.

And the accumulated splashing of a gong
where tissue plunges into bronze with wide wild circles of
    sound and leaves off,
belongs to the bamboo thickets, and the drake in the air
    flying past.

And the sound of a blast through the sea-curved core of a
    shell
when a black priest blows on a conch,
and the dawn-cry from a minaret, God is Great,
and the calling of the old Red Indian high on the pueblo
    roof
whose voice flies on and on, calling like a swan
singing between the sun and the marsh,
on and on, like a dark-faced bird singing alone
singing to the men below, the fellow-tribesmen
who go by without pausing, soft-foot, without listening,
    yet who hear:
there are other ways of summons, crying: Listen! Listen!
    Come near!

THE TRIUMPH OF THE MACHINE

THEY talk of the triumph of the machine,
but the machine will never triumph.

Out of the thousands and thousands of centuries of man
the unrolling of ferns, white tongues of the acanthus lap-
　　ping at the sun,
for one sad century
machines have triumphed, rolled us hither and thither,
shaking the lark's nest till the eggs have broken.
Shaken the marshes till the geese have gone
and the wild swans flown away singing the swan-song of
　　us.

Hard, hard on the earth the machines are rolling,
but through some hearts they will never roll.

The lark nests in his heart
and the white swan swims in the marshes of his loins,
and through the wide prairies of his breast a young bull
　　herds his cows,
lambs frisk among the daisies of his brain.

And at last
all these creatures that cannot die, driven back
into the uttermost corners of the soul,
will send up the wild cry of despair.

The trilling lark in a wild despair will trill down arrows
　　from the sky,
the swan will beat the waters in rage, white rage of an
　　enraged swan,
even the lambs will stretch forth their necks like serpents,
like snakes of hate, against the man in the machine:
even the shaking white poplar will dazzle like splinters of
　　glass against him.

And against this inward revolt of the native creatures of
　　the soul
mechanical man, in triumph seated upon the seat of his
　　machine

will be powerless, for no engine can reach into the marshes
and depths of a man.

So mechanical man in triumph seated upon the seat of his
machine
will be driven mad from within himself, and sightless, and
on that day
the machines will turn to run into one another
traffic will tangle up in a long-drawn-out crash of collision
and engines will rush at the solid houses, the edifice of our
life
will rock in the shock of the mad machine, and the house
will come down.

Then, far beyond the ruin, in the far, in the ultimate,
remote places
the swan will lift up again his flattened, smitten head
and look round, and rise, and on the great vaults of his
wings
will sweep round and up to greet the sun with a silky
glitter of a new day
and the lark will follow trilling, angerless again,
and the lambs will bite off the heads of the daisies for very
friskiness.
But over the middle of the earth will be the smoky ruin of
iron
the triumph of the machine.

WE DIE TOGETHER

Oh, when I think of the industrial millions, when I see
some of them,
a weight comes over me heavier than leaden linings of
coffins
and I almost cease to exist, weighed down to extinction
and sunk into a depression that almost blots me out.

Then I say to myself: Am I also dead? is that the truth?
Then I know
that with so many dead men in mills
I too am almost dead.
I know the unliving factory-hand, living-dead millions
is unliving me, living-dead me,
I, with them, am living-dead, mechanical at the machine.

And enshrouded in the vast corpse of the industrial
        millions
embedded in them, I look out on the sunshine of the South.

And though the pomegranate has red flowers outside the
        window
and oleander is hot with perfume under the afternoon sun
and I am 'il Signore' and they love me here,
yet I am a mill-hand in Leeds
and the death of the Black Country is upon me
and I am wrapped in the lead of a coffin-lining, the living
        death of my fellow men.

INNOCENT ENGLAND

Oh what a pity, Oh! don't you agree
that figs aren't found in the land of the free!

Fig-trees don't grow in my native land;
there's never a fig-leaf near at hand

when you want one; so I did without;
and that is what the row's about.

Virginal, pure policemen came
and hid their faces for very shame,

while they carried the shameless things away
to gaol, to be hid from the light of day.

And Mr Mead, that old, old lily
said: 'Gross! coarse! hideous!' – and I, like a silly

thought he meant the faces of the police-court officials,
and how right he was, and I signed my initials

to confirm what he said; but alas, he meant
my pictures, and on the proceedings went.

The upshot was, my picture must burn
that English artists might finally learn

when they painted a nude, to put a *cache sexe* on,
a cache sexe, a cache sexe, or else begone!

A fig leaf; or, if you cannot find it
a wreath of mist, with nothing behind it.

A wreath of mist is the usual thing
in the north, to hide where the turtles sing.

Though they never sing, they never sing,
don't you dare to suggest such a thing

or Mr Mead will be after you.
– But what a pity I never knew

A wreath of English mist would do
as a cache sexe! I'd have put a whole fog.

But once and forever barks the old dog,
so my pictures are in prison, instead of in the Zoo.

MODERN PRAYER

ALMIGHTY Mammon, make me rich!
Make me rich quickly, with never a hitch
in my fine prosperity! Kick those in the ditch
who hinder me, Mammon, great son of a bitch!

LEAVES OF GRASS, FLOWERS OF GRASS

Leaves of grass, what about leaves of grass?
Grass blossoms, grass has flowers, flowers of grass
dusty pollen of grass, tall grass in its midsummer maleness,
hay-seed and tiny grain of grass, graminiferae
not far from the lily, the considerable lily;

even the blue-grass blossoms;
even the bison knew it;
even the stupidest farmer gathers his hay in bloom, in
blossom
just before it seeds.

Only the best matters; even the cow knows it;
grass in blossom, blossoming grass, risen to its height and
its natural pride
in its own splendour and its own feathery maleness
the grass, the grass.

Leaves of grass, what are leaves of grass, when at its best
grass blossoms.

STORM IN THE BLACK FOREST

Now it is almost night, from the bronzey soft sky
jugfull after jugfull of pure white liquid fire, bright white
tipples over and spills down,
and is gone
and gold-bronze flutters bent through the thick upper air.

And as the electric liquid pours out, sometimes
a still brighter white snake wriggles among it, spilled
and tumbling wriggling down the sky:
and then the heavens cackle with uncouth sounds.

And the rain won't come, the rain refuses to come!

This is the electricity that man is supposed to have mas-
    tered
chained, subjugated to his use!
supposed to!

NAME THE GODS!

I REFUSE to name the gods, because they have no name.
I refuse to describe the gods, because they have no form
    nor shape nor substance.

Ah, but the simple ask for images!
Then for a time at least, they must do without.

But all the time I see the gods:
the man who is mowing the tall white corn,
suddenly, as it curves, as it yields, the white wheat
and sinks down with a swift rustle, and a strange, falling
    flatness,
ah! the gods, the swaying body of god!
ah the fallen stillness of god, autumnus, and it is only July
the pale-gold flesh of Priapus dropping asleep.

THERE ARE NO GODS

THERE are no gods, and you can please yourself
have a game of tennis, go out in the car, do some shopping,
    sit and talk, talk, talk
with a cigarette browning your fingers.

There are no gods, and you can please yourself –
go and please yourself –

But leave me alone, leave me alone, to myself!
and then in the room, whose is the presence
that makes the air so still and lovely to me?

Who is it that softly touches the sides of my breast
and touches me over the heart
so that my heart beats soothed, soothed, soothed and at
    peace?

Who is it smooths the bed-sheets like the cool
smooth ocean where the fishes rest on edge
in their own dream?

Who is it that clasps and kneads my naked feet, till they
    unfold,
till all is well, till all is utterly well? the lotus-lilies of the
    feet!

I tell you, it is no woman, it is no man, for I am alone.
And I fall asleep with the gods, the gods
that are not, or that are
according to the soul's desire,
like a pool into which we plunge, or do not plunge.

RETORT TO WHITMAN

AND whoever walks a mile full of false sympathy
walks to the funeral of the whole human race.

RETORT TO JESUS

AND whoever forces himself to love anybody
begets a murderer in his own body.

TERRA INCOGNITA

THERE are vast realms of consciousness still undreamed of
vast ranges of experience, like the humming of unseen
    harps,
we know nothing of, within us.

Oh when man has escaped from the barbed-wire entangle-
ment
of his own ideas and his own mechanical devices
there is a marvellous rich world of contact and sheer fluid
beauty
and fearless face-to-face awareness of now-naked life
and me, and you, and other men and women
and grapes, and ghouls, and ghosts and green moonlight
and ruddy-orange limbs stirring the limbo
of the unknown air, and eyes so soft
softer than the space between the stars,
and all things, and nothing, and being and not-being
alternately palpitant;
when at last we escape the barbed-wire enclosure
of *Know Thyself*, knowing we can never know,
we can but touch, and wonder, and ponder, and make our
effort
and dangle in a last fastidious fine delight
as the fuchsia does, dangling her reckless drop
of purple after so much putting forth
and slow mounting marvel of a little tree.

FOR A MOMENT

FOR a moment, at evening, tired, as he stepped off the
tram-car,
— the young tram-conductor in a blue uniform, to
himself forgotten, —
and lifted his face up, with blue eyes looking at the electric
rod which he was going to turn round,
for a moment, pure in the yellow evening light, he was
Hyacinthus.

In the green garden darkened the shadow of coming rain
and a girl ran swiftly, laughing breathless, taking in her
white washing

in rapid armfuls from the line, tossing it in the basket,
and so rapidly, and so flashing, fleeing before the rain
for a moment she was Io, Io, who fled from Zeus, or the
    Danaë.

When I was waiting and not thinking, sitting at a table on
    the hotel terrace
I saw suddenly coming towards me, lit up and uplifted
    with pleasure
advancing with the slow-swiftness of a ship backing her
    white sails into port
the woman who looks for me in the world
and for the moment she was Isis, gleaming, having found
    her Osiris.

For a moment, as he looked at me through his spectacles
pondering, yet eager, the broad and thick-set Italian who
    works in with me,
for a moment he was the Centaur, the wise yet horse-
    hoofed Centaur
in whom I can trust.

THOUGHT

THOUGHT, I love thought.
But not the jiggling and twisting of already existent ideas
I despise that self-important game.
Thought is the welling up of unknown life into conscious-
    ness,
Thought is the testing of statements on the touchstone of
    the conscience,
Thought is gazing on to the face of life, and reading what
    can be read,
Thought is pondering over experience, and coming to a
    conclusion.
Thought is not a trick, or an exercise, or a set of dodges,
Thought is a man in his wholeness wholly attending.

GOD IS BORN

THE history of the cosmos
is the history of the struggle of becoming.
When the dim flux of unformed life
struggled, convulsed back and forth upon itself,
and broke at last into light and dark
came into existence as light,
came into existence as cold shadow
then every atom of the cosmos trembled with delight.
Behold, God is born!
He is bright light!
He is pitch dark and cold!

And in the great struggle of intangible chaos
when, at a certain point, a drop of water began to drip
    downwards
and a breath of vapour began to wreathe up
Lo again the shudder of bliss through all the atoms!
Oh, God is born!
Behold, he is born wet!
Look, He hath movement upward! He spirals!

And so, in the great aeons of accomplishment and débâcle
from time to time the wild crying of every electron:
Lo! God is born!

When sapphires cooled out of molten chaos:
See, God is born! He is blue, he is deep blue, he is forever
    blue!
When gold lay shining threading the cooled-off rock:
God is born! God is born! bright yellow and ductile He is
    born.

When the little eggy amoeba emerged out of foam and
    nowhere

then all the electrons held their breath:
Ach! Ach! Now indeed God is born! He twinkles within.

When from a world of mosses and of ferns
at last the narcissus lifted a tuft of five-point stars
and dangled them in the atmosphere,
then every molecule of creation jumped and clapped its
    hands:
God is born! God is born perfumed and dangling and with
    a little cup!

Throughout the aeons, as the lizard swirls his tail finer
    than water,
as the peacock turns to the sun, and could not be more
    splendid,
as the leopard smites the small calf with a spangled paw,
    perfect.
the universe trembles: God is born! God is here!

And when at last man stood on two legs and wondered,
then there was a hush of suspense at the core of every
    electron:
Behold, now very God is born!
God Himself is born!

And so we see, God is not
until he is born.

And also we see
there is no end to the birth of God.

FLOWERS AND MEN

FLOWERS achieve their own floweriness and it is a miracle.
Men don't achieve their own manhood, alas, oh alas! alas!

All I want of you, men and women,
all I want of you

229

is that you shall achieve your own beauty
as the flowers do.

Oh leave off saying I want you to be savages.
Tell me, is the gentian savage, at the top of its coarse stem?
Oh what in you can answer to this blueness?

FIRE

DID you ever warm your hands at the combustion of
carbon and oxygen, or glow in the face from the
formation of carbon dioxide by means of combustion?
What do you see there, then, as the twigs crackle and
the gold rushes out and ripples flapping brilliant to a peak
of gold within the smoke? What is it then that lies red,
and writhes a little, changes upon itself, glows upon
you, gladdens the blood, faintly withdraws. What is it?
Oh lovely Fire, what is it but you, lovely Fire, that was
not and is, to my joy. Oh lovely fire on this chill day,
as the sun goes down, I ask not how you nest and
crackle so red, with pinions of swift gold, among the
moving transfigured twigs! I ask not how nor whence
nor whither, for if I ask I shall only answer myself with a
thousand damp equivocations. I only ask that you shall
be with me, bright, rustling, fierce-fanged fire, I only
delight in your companionship that is nakeder and more
interpenetrating than love, swift, swift ruddy one
feathered with gold, that eludes every question forever.
Elude then, elude their cold and mean little questions,
these pale-lipped be-spectacled men! But for me, Oh again
I am a wine-cup, and my chill heart is empty of wine. Oh
pour, pour, pour into the vessels of my heart, run in
through the branched hands, hover like a butterfly ruddy
on the cheeks that were chill, pulsing them with brilliant

warmth, beautiful fire, beautiful fire, joy of my soul in this twilight, now the sun has gone and the blue shadow is thinking of hoar-frost, outside the house. But I am before the fire, and my heart is open.

Last Poems

THE ARGONAUTS

THEY are not dead, they are not dead!
Now that the sun, like a lion licks his paws
and goes slowly down the hill:
now that the moon, who remembers, and only cares
that we should be lovely in the flesh, with bright, crescent
        feet,
pauses near the crest of the hill, climbing slowly, like a
        queen
looking down on the lion as he retreats –

Now the sea is the Argonauts' sea, and in the dawn
Odysseus calls the commands, as he steers past those
        foamy islands;
wait, wait, don't bring me the coffee yet, nor the *pain grillé*.
The dawn is not off the sea, and Odysseus' ships
have not yet passed the islands, I must watch them still.

MIDDLE OF THE WORLD

THIS sea will never die, neither will it ever grow old
nor cease to be blue, nor in the dawn
cease to lift up its hills
and let the slim black ship of Dionysos come sailing in
with grape-vines up the mast, and dolphins leaping.

What do I care if the smoking ships
of the P. & O. and the Orient Line and all the other stinkers
cross like clock-work the Minoan distance!
They only cross, the distance never changes.

And now that the moon who gives men glistening bodies
is in her exaltation, and can look down on the sun
I see descending from the ships at dawn

slim naked men from Cnossos, smiling the archaic smile
of those that will without fail come back again,
and kindling little fires upon the shores
and crouching, and speaking the music of lost languages.

And the Minoan Gods, and the Gods of Tiryns
are heard softly laughing and chatting, as ever;
and Dionysos, young and a stranger
leans listening on the gate, in all respect.

FOR THE HEROES ARE DIPPED IN SCARLET

BEFORE Plato told the great lie of ideals
men slimly went like fishes, and didn't care.

They had long hair, like Samson,
and clean as arrows they sped at the mark
when the bow-cord twanged.

They knew it was no use knowing
their own nothingness:
for they were not nothing.

So now they come back! Hark!
Hark! the low and shattering laughter of bearded men
with the slim waists of warriors, and the long feet
of moon-lit dancers.

Oh, and their faces scarlet, like the dolphin's blood!
Lo! the loveliest is red all over, rippling vermilion
as he ripples upwards!
laughing in his black beard!

They are dancing! they return, as they went, dancing!
For the thing that is done without the glowing as of god,
    vermilion,
were best not done at all.
How glistening red they are!

DEMIURGE

THEY say that reality exists only in the spirit
that corporal existence is a kind of death
that pure being is bodiless
that the idea of the form precedes the form substantial.

But what nonsense it is!
as if any Mind could have imagined a lobster
dozing in the under-deeps, then reaching out a savage and
     iron claw!

Even the mind of God can only imagine
those things that have become themselves:
bodies and presences, here and now, creatures with a
     foothold in creation
even if it is only a lobster on tip-toe.

Religion knows better than philosophy.
Religion knows that Jesus was never Jesus
till he was born from a womb, and ate soup and bread
and grew up, and became, in the wonder of creation, Jesus,
with a body and with needs, and a lovely spirit.

RED GERANIUM AND GODLY MIGNONETTE

IMAGINE that any mind ever *thought* a red geranium!
As if the redness of a red geranium could be anything but a
     sensual experience
and as if sensual experience could take place before there
     were any senses.
We know that even God could not imagine the redness of
     a red geranium
nor the smell of mignonette
when geraniums were not, and mignonette neither.
And even when they were, even God would have to have
     a nose to smell at the mignonette.

You can't imagine the Holy Ghost sniffing at cherry-pie
    heliotrope.
Or the Most High, during the coal age, cudgelling his
    mighty brains
even if he had any brains: straining his mighty mind
to think, among the moss and mud of lizards and masto-
    dons
to think out, in the abstract, when all was twilit green and
    muddy:
'Now there shall be tum-tiddly-um, and tum-tiddly-um,
hey-presto! scarlet geranium!'
We know it couldn't be done.

But imagine, among the mud and the mastodons
God sighing and yearning with tremendous creative yearn-
    ing, in that dark green mess
oh, for some other beauty, some other beauty
that blossomed at last, red geranium, and mignonette.

THE BODY OF GOD

GOD is the great urge that has not yet found a body
but urges towards incarnation with the great creative urge.

And becomes at last a clove carnation: lo! that is god!
and becomes at last Helen, or Ninon: any lovely and
    generous woman
at her best and her most beautiful, being god, made mani-
    fest,
any clear and fearless man being god, very god.

There is no god
apart from poppies and the flying fish,
men singing songs, and women brushing their hair in the
    sun.

The lovely things are god that has come to pass, like Jesus
    came.
The rest, the undiscoverable, is the demi-urge.

THE RAINBOW

EVEN the rainbow has a body
made of the drizzling rain
and is an architecture of glistening atoms
built up, built up
yet you can't lay your hand on it,
nay, nor even your mind.

THE MAN OF TYRE

THE man of Tyre went down to the sea
pondering, for he was Greek, that God is one and all alone
    and ever more shall be so.
And a woman who had been washing clothes in the pool
    of rock
where a stream came down to the gravel of the sea and
    sank in,
who had spread white washing on the gravel banked
    above the bay,
who had lain her shift on the shore, on the shingle slope,
who had waded to the pale green sea of evening, out to a
    shoal,
pouring sea-water over herself
now turned, and came slowly back, with her back to the
    evening sky.

Oh lovely, lovely with the dark hair piled up, as she went
    deeper, deeper down the channel, then rose shallower,
    shallower,
with the full thighs slowly lifting of the wader wading
    shorewards

and the shoulders pallid with light from the silent sky
    behind
both breasts dim and mysterious, with the glamorous
    kindness of twilight between them
and the dim blotch of black maidenhair like an indicator,
giving a message to the man –

So in the cane-brake he clasped his hands in delight
that could only be god-given, and murmured:
Lo! God is one god! But here in the twilight
godly and lovely comes Aphrodite out of the sea
towards me!

THEY SAY THE SEA IS LOVELESS

THEY say the sea is loveless, that in the sea
love cannot live, but only bare, salt splinters
of loveless life.
But from the sea
the dolphins leap round Dionysos' ship
whose masts have purple vines,
and up they come with the purple dark of rainbows
and flip! they go! with the nose-dive of sheer delight:
and the sea is making love to Dionysos
in the bouncing of these small and happy whales.

WHALES WEEP NOT!

THEY say the sea is cold, but the sea contains
the hottest blood of all, and the wildest, the most urgent.

All the whales in the wider deeps, hot are they, as they urge
on and on, and dive beneath the icebergs.
The right whales, the sperm-whales, the hammer-heads,
    the killers

there they blow, there they blow, hot wild white breath
out of the sea!

And they rock, and they rock, through the sensual ageless
ages
on the depths of the seven seas,
and through the salt they reel with drunk delight
and in the tropics tremble they with love
and roll with massive, strong desire, like gods.
Then the great bull lies up against his bride
in the blue deep bed of the sea,
as mountain pressing on mountain, in the zest of life:
and out of the inward roaring of the inner red ocean of
whale-blood
the long tip reaches strong, intense, like the maelstrom-tip,
and comes to rest
in the clasp and the soft, wild clutch of a she-whale's
fathomless body.

And over the bridge of the whale's strong phallus, linking
the wonder of whales
the burning archangels under the sea keep passing, back
and forth,
keep passing, archangels of bliss
from him to her, from her to him, great Cherubim
that wait on whales in mid-ocean, suspended in the waves
of the sea
great heaven of whales in the waters, old hierarchies.

And enormous mother whales lie dreaming suckling their
whale-tender young
and dreaming with strange whale eyes wide open in the
waters of the beginning and the end.

And bull-whales gather their women and whale-calves in a
ring

when danger threatens, on the surface of the ceaseless flood
and range themselves like great fierce Seraphim facing the
    threat
encircling their huddled monsters of love.
And all this happens in the sea, in the salt
where God is also love, but without words:
and Aphrodite is the wife of whales
most happy, happy she!

and Venus among the fishes skips and is a she-dolphin
she is the gay, delighted porpoise sporting with love and
    the sea
she is the female tunny-fish, round and happy among the
    males
and dense with happy blood, dark rainbow bliss in the sea.

INVOCATION TO THE MOON

You beauty, O you beauty
you glistening garmentless beauty!
great lady, great glorious lady
greatest of ladies
crownless and jewelless and garmentless
because naked you are more wonderful than anything we
    can stroke –

Be good to me, lady, great lady of the nearest
heavenly mansion, and last!
Now I am at your gate, you beauty, you lady of all
    nakedness!
Now I must enter your mansion, and beg your gift
Moon, O Moon, great lady of the heavenly few.

Far and forgotten is the Villa of Venus the glowing
and behind me now in the gulfs of space lies the golden
    house of the sun,

and six have given me gifts, and kissed me god-speed
kisses of four great lords, beautiful, as they held me to their
      bosom in farewell
and kiss of the far-off lingering lady who looks over the
      distant fence of the twilight,
and one warm kind kiss of the lion with golden paws –

Now, lady of the Moon, now open the gate of your silvery
      house
and let me come past the silver bells of your flowers, and
      the cockle-shells
into your house, garmentless lady of the last great gift:
who will give me back my lost limbs
and my lost white fearless breast
and set me again on moon-remembering feet
a healed, whole man, O Moon!

Lady, lady of the last house down the long, long street of
      the stars
be good to me now, as I beg you, as you've always been
      good to men
who begged of you and gave you homage
and watched for your glistening feet down the garden path!

BUTTERFLY

BUTTERFLY, the wind blows sea-ward, strong beyond the
      garden wall!
Butterfly, why do you settle on my shoe, and sip the dirt
      on my shoe,
lifting your veined wings, lifting them? big white butterfly!

Already it is October, and the wind blows strong to the sea
from the hills where snow must have fallen, the wind is
      polished with snow.

Here in the garden, with red geraniums, it is warm, it is
    warm
but the wind blows strong to sea-ward, white butterfly,
    content on my shoe!

Will you go, will you go from my warm house?
Will you climb on your big soft wings, black-dotted,
as up an invisible rainbow, an arch
till the wind slides you sheer from the arch-crest
and in a strange level fluttering you go out to sea-ward,
    white speck!

Farewell, farewell, lost soul!
you have melted in the crystalline distance,
it is enough! I saw you vanish into air.

BAVARIAN GENTIANS

Not every man has gentians in his house
in soft September, at slow, sad Michaelmas.
Bavarian gentians, tall and dark, but dark
darkening the daytime torch-like with the smoking blueness
    of Pluto's gloom,
ribbed hellish flowers erect, with their blaze of darkness
    spread blue,
blown flat into points, by the heavy white draught of the
    day.

Torch-flowers of the blue-smoking darkness, Pluto's
    dark-blue blaze
black lamps from the halls of Dis, smoking dark blue
giving off darkness, blue darkness, upon Demeter's
    yellow-pale day
whom have you come for, here in the white-cast day?

Reach me a gentian, give me a torch!
let me guide myself with the blue, forked torch of a flower
down the darker and darker stairs, where blue is darkened
    on blueness
down the way Persephone goes, just now, in first-frosted
    September,
to the sightless realm where darkness is married to dark
and Persephone herself is but a voice, as a bride,
a gloom invisible enfolded in the deeper dark
of the arms of Pluto as he ravishes her once again
and pierces her once more with his passion of the utter dark
among the splendour of black-blue torches, shedding
    fathomless darkness on the nuptials.

Give me a flower on a tall stem, and three dark flames,
for I will go to the wedding, and be wedding-guest
at the marriage of the living dark.

LUCIFER

ANGELS are bright still, though the brightest fell.
But tell me, tell me, how do you know
he lost any of his brightness in the falling?
In the dark-blue depths, under layers and layers of
    darkness,
I see him move like the ruby, a gleam from within
of his own magnificence,
coming like the ruby in the invisible dark, glowing
with his own annunciation, towards us.

PAX

ALL that matters is to be at one with the living God
to be a creature in the house of the God of Life.

Like a cat asleep on a chair
at peace, in peace
and at one with the master of the house, with the mistress,
at home, at home in the house of the living,
sleeping on the hearth, and yawning before the fire.

Sleeping on the hearth of the living world
yawning at home before the fire of life
feeling the presence of the living God
like a great reassurance
a deep calm in the heart
a presence
as of the master sitting at the board
in his own and greater being,
in the house of life.

ONLY MAN

ONLY man can fall from God
Only man.

No animal, no beast nor creeping thing
no cobra nor hyaena nor scorpion nor hideous white ant
can slip entirely through the fingers of the hands of god
into the abyss of self-knowledge,
knowledge of the self-apart-from-god.

For the knowledge of the self-apart-from-God
is an abyss down which the soul can slip
writhing and twisting in all the revolutions
of the unfinished plunge
of self-awareness, now apart from God, falling
fathomless, fathomless, self-consciousness wriggling
writhing deeper and deeper in all the minutiae of self-
    knowledge, downwards, exhaustive,
yet never, never coming to the bottom, for there is no
    bottom;

zigzagging down like the fizzle from a finished rocket
the frizzling falling fire that cannot go out, dropping
    wearily,
neither can it reach the depth
for the depth is bottomless,
so it wriggles its way even further down, further down
at last in sheer horror of not being able to leave off
knowing itself, knowing itself apart from God, falling.

IN THE CITIES

In the cities
there is even no more any weather
the weather in town is always benzine, or else petrol fumes
lubricating oil, exhaust gas.

As over some dense marsh, the fumes
thicken, miasma, the fumes of the automobile
densely thicken in the cities.

In ancient Rome, down the thronged streets
no wheels might run, no insolent chariots.
Only the footsteps, footsteps
of people
and the gentle trotting of the litter-bearers.

In Minos, in Mycenae
in all the cities with lion gates
the dead threaded the air, lingering
lingering in the earth's shadow
and leaning towards the old hearth.

In London, New York, Paris
in the bursten cities
the dead tread heavily through the muddy air
through the mire of fumes
heavily, stepping weary on our hearts.

For thine is the kingdom
the power, and the glory —

Hallowed by thy name, then
Thou who art nameless —

Give me, Oh give me
besides my daily bread
my kingdom, my power, and my glory.

All things that turn to thee
have their kingdom, their power, and their glory.

Like the kingdom of the nightingale at twilight
whose power and glory I have often heard and felt.

Like the kingdom of the fox in the dark
yapping in his power and his glory
which is death to the goose.

Like the power and the glory of the goose in the mist
honking over the lake.

And I, a naked man, calling
calling to thee for my mana,
my kingdom, my power, and my glory.

MANA OF THE SEA

Do you see the sea, breaking itself to bits against the islands
yet remaining unbroken, the level great sea?

Have I caught from it
the tide in my arms
that runs down to the shallows of my wrists, and breaks
abroad in my hands, like waves among the rocks of sub-
    stance?

Do the rollers of the sea
roll down my thighs
and over the submerged islets of my knees
with power, sea-power
sea-power
to break against the ground
in the flat, recurrent breakers of my two feet?

And is my body ocean, ocean
whose power runs to the shores along my arms
and breaks in the foamy hands, whose power rolls out
to the white-treading waves of two salt feet?

I am the sea, I am the sea!

ANAXAGORAS

WHEN Anaxagoras says: Even snow is black!
he is taken by the scientists very seriously
because he is enunciating a 'principle', a 'law'
that all things are mixed, and therefore the purest white
    snow
has in it an element of blackness.

That they call science, and reality.
I call it mental conceit and mystification
and nonsense, for pure snow is white to us
white and white and only white
with a lovely bloom of whiteness upon white
in which the soul delights and the senses
have an experience of bliss.

And life is for delight, and for bliss
and dread, and the dark, rolling ominousness of doom.
Then the bright dawning of delight again
from off the sheer white snow, or the poised moon.

And in the shadow of the sun the snow is blue, so blue-
aloof
with a hint of the frozen bells of the scylla flower
but never the ghost of a glimpse of Anaxagoras' funeral
black.

KISSING AND HORRID STRIFE

I HAVE been defeated and dragged down by pain
and worsted by the evil world-soul of today.

But still I know that life is for delight
and for bliss
as now when the tiny wavelets of the sea
tip the morning light on edge, and spill it with delight
to show how inexhaustible it is.

And life is for delight, and bliss
like now when the white sun kisses the sea
and plays with the wavelets like a panther playing with its
cubs
cuffing them with soft paws,
and blows that are caresses,
kisses of the soft-balled paws, where the talons are.

And life is for dread,
for doom that darkens, and the Sunderers
that sunder us from each other,
that strip us and destroy us and break us down
as the tall foxgloves and the mulleins and mallows
are torn down by dismembering autumn
till not a vestige is left, and black winter has no trace
of any such flowers;
and yet the roots below the blackness are intact:
the Thunderers and the Sunderers have their term,
their limit, their thus far and no further.

Life is for kissing and for horrid strife.
Life is for the angels and the Sunderers,
Life is for the daimons and the demons,
those that put honey on our lips, and those that put salt.
But life is not
for the dead vanity of knowing better, nor the blank
cold comfort of superiority, nor silly
conceit of being immune,
nor puerility of contradictions
like saying snow is black, or desire is evil.

Life is for kissing and for horrid strife,
the angels and the Sunderers.
And perhaps in unknown Death we perhaps shall know
Oneness and poised immunity.
But why then should we die while we can live?
And while we live
the kissing and communing cannot cease
nor yet the striving and the horrid strife.

WHEN SATAN FELL

WHEN Satan fell, he only fell
because the Lord Almighty rose a bit too high,
a bit beyond himself.

So Satan only fell to keep a balance.
'Are you so lofty, O my God?
Are you so pure and lofty, up aloft?
Then I will fall, and plant the paths to hell
with vines and poppies and fig-trees
so that lost souls may eat grapes
and the moist fig
and put scarlet buds in their hair on the way to hell,
on the way to dark perdition.'

And hell and heaven are the scales of the balance of life
which swing against each other.

DEATH IS NOT EVIL, EVIL IS MECHANICAL

ONLY the human being, absolved from kissing and strife
goes on and on and on, without wandering
fixed upon the hub of the ego
going, yet never wandering, fixed, yet in motion,
the kind of hell that is real, grey and awful
sinless and stainless going round and round
the kind of hell grey Dante never saw
but of which he had a bit inside him.

Know thyself, and that thou art mortal.
But know thyself, denying that thou art mortal:
a thing of kisses and strife
a lit-up shaft of rain
a calling column of blood
a rose tree bronzey with thorns
a mixture of yea and nay
a rainbow of love and hate
a wind that blows back and forth
a creature of beautiful peace, like a river
and a creature of conflict, like a cataract:
know thyself, in denial of all these things –

And thou shalt begin to spin round on the hub of the
        obscene ego
a grey void thing that goes without wandering
a machine that in itself is nothing
a centre of the evil world-soul.

THE SHIP OF DEATH

1

Now it is autumn and the falling fruit
and the long journey towards oblivion.

The apples falling like great drops of dew
to bruise themselves an exit from themselves.

And it is time to go, to bid farewell
to one's own self, and find an exit
from the fallen self.

2

Have you built your ship of death, O have you?
O build your ship of death, for you will need it.

The grim frost is at hand, when the apples will fall
thick, almost thundrous, on the hardened earth.

And death is on the air like a smell of ashes!
Ah! can't you smell it?

And in the bruised body, the frightened soul
finds itself shrinking, wincing from the cold
that blows upon it through the orifices.

3

And can a man his own quietus make
with a bare bodkin?

With daggers, bodkins, bullets, man can make
a bruise or break of exit for his life;
but is that a quietus, O tell me, is it quietus?

Surely not so! for how could murder, even self-murder
ever a quietus make?

O let us talk of quiet that we know,
that we can know, the deep and lovely quiet
of a strong heart at peace!

How can we this, our own quietus, make?

5

Build then the ship of death, for you must take
the longest journey, to oblivion.

And die the death, the long and painful death
that lies between the old self and the new.

Already our bodies are fallen, bruised, badly bruised,
already our souls are oozing through the exit
of the cruel bruise.

Already the dark and endless ocean of the end
is washing in through the breaches of our wounds,
already the flood is upon us.

Oh build your ship of death, your little ark
and furnish it with food, with little cakes, and wine
for the dark flight down oblivion.

Piecemeal the body dies, and the timid soul
has her footing washed away, as the dark flood rises.

We are dying, we are dying, we are all of us dying
and nothing will stay the death-flood rising within us
and soon it will rise on the world, on the outside world.

We are dying, we are dying, piecemeal our bodies are dying
and our strength leaves us,
and our soul cowers naked in the dark rain over the flood,
cowering in the last branches of the tree of our life.

We are dying, we are dying, so all we can do
is now to be willing to die, and to build the ship
of death to carry the soul on the longest journey.

A little ship, with oars and food
and little dishes, and all accoutrements
fitting and ready for the departing soul.

Now launch the small ship, now as the body dies
and life departs, launch out, the fragile soul
in the fragile ship of courage, the ark of faith
with its store of food and little cooking pans
and change of clothes,
upon the flood's black waste
upon the waters of the end
upon the sea of death, where still we sail
darkly, for we cannot steer, and have no port.

There is no port, there is nowhere to go
only the deepening blackness darkening still
blacker upon the soundless, ungurgling flood
darkness at one with darkness, up and down
and sideways utterly dark, so there is no direction any more.
And the little ship is there; yet she is gone.
She is not seen, for there is nothing to see her by.
She is gone! gone! and yet
somewhere she is there.
Nowhere!

8

And everything is gone, the body is gone
completely under, gone, entirely gone.
The upper darkness is heavy as the lower,
between them the little ship
is gone

she is gone.

It is the end, it is oblivion.

9

And yet out of eternity, a thread
separates itself on the blackness,
a horizontal thread
that fumes a little with pallor upon the dark.

Is it illusion? or does the pallor fume
A little higher?
Ah wait, wait, for there's the dawn,
the cruel dawn of coming back to life
out of oblivion.

Wait, wait, the little ship
drifting, beneath the deathly ashy grey
of a flood-dawn.

Wait, wait! even so, a flush of yellow
and strangely, O chilled wan soul, a flush of rose.

A flush of rose, and the whole thing starts again.

10

The flood subsides, and the body, like a worn sea-shell
emerges strange and lovely.
And the little ship wings home, faltering and lapsing
on the pink flood,
and the frail soul steps out, into her house again
filling the heart with peace.

Swings the heart renewed with peace
even of oblivion.

Oh build your ship of death, oh build it!
for you will need it.
For the voyage of oblivion awaits you.

SHADOWS

AND if tonight my soul may find her peace
in sleep, and sink in good oblivion,
and in the morning wake like a new-opened flower
then I have been dipped again in God, and new-created.

And if, as weeks go round, in the dark of the moon
my spirit darkens and goes out, and soft, strange gloom
pervades my movements and my thoughts and words
then I shall know that I am walking still
with God, we are close together now the moon's in
shadow.

And if, as autumn deepens and darkens
I feel the pain of falling leaves, and stems that break in
storms
and trouble and dissolution and distress
and then the softness of deep shadows folding, folding
around my soul and spirit, around my lips
so sweet, like a swoon, or more like the drowse of a low,
sad song
singing darker than the nightingale, on, on to the solstice
and the silence of short days, the silence of the year, the
shadow,
then I shall know that my life is moving still
with the dark earth, and drenched
with the deep oblivion of earth's lapse and renewal.

And if, in the changing phases of man's life
I fall in sickness and in misery
my wrists seem broken and my heart seems dead
and strength is gone, and my life
is only the leavings of a life:

and still, among it all, snatches of lovely oblivion, and
snatches of renewal

odd, wintry flowers upon the withered stem, yet new
    strange flowers
such as my life has not brought forth before, new blossoms
    of me –

then I must know that still
I am in the hands of the unknown God,
he is breaking me down to his own oblivion
to send me forth on a new morning, a new man.

INDEX OF TITLES

MORE ABOUT PENGUINS
AND PELICANS

Penguinews, which appears every month, contains details of all the new books issued by Penguins as they are published. From time to time it is supplemented by the *Penguin Stock List*, which is our complete list of almost 5,000 titles.

A specimen copy of *Penguinews* will be sent to you free on request. Please write to Dept EP, Penguin Books Ltd, Harmondsworth, Middlesex, for your copy.

In the U.S.A.: For a complete list of books available from Penguins in the United States write to Dept CS, Penguin Books, 625 Madison Avenue, New York, New York 10022.

In Canada: For a complete list of books available from Penguins in Canada write to Penguin Books Canada Ltd, 2801 John Street, Markham, Ontario L3R 1B4.

D. H. LAWRENCE IN PENGUINS

D. H. Lawrence is now acknowledged as one of the greatest writers of the twentieth century. Nearly all his works have been published in Penguins:

Novels

AARON'S ROD
LADY CHATTERLEY'S LOVER
THE LOST GIRL
THE PLUMED SERPENT
THE RAINBOW
SONS AND LOVERS
THE TRESPASSER
THE WHITE PEACOCK
WOMEN IN LOVE
KANGAROO
THE FIRST LADY CHATTERLEY
JOHN THOMAS AND LADY JANE

Short Stories

PRUSSIAN OFFICER
ENGLAND, MY ENGLAND
LOVE AMONG THE HAYSTACKS
THE WOMAN WHO RODE AWAY
THREE NOVELLAS: THE FOX, THE LADYBIRD, THE CAPTAIN'S DOLL
ST MAWR *and* THE VIRGIN AND THE GIPSY
THE PRINCESS AND OTHER STORIES
THE MORTAL COIL AND OTHER STORIES
THE VIRGIN AND THE GIPSY

Travel Books and Other Works

APOCALYPSE
MORNINGS IN MEXICO *and* ETRUSCAN PLACES
SEA AND SARDINIA
TWILIGHT IN ITALY
SELECTED ESSAYS
FANTASIA OF THE UNCONSCIOUS *and* PSYCHOANALYSIS AND THE UNCONSCIOUS